Edward Maitland

By and By

Vol. 3

Edward Maitland

By and By
Vol. 3

ISBN/EAN: 9783337346799

Printed in Europe, USA, Canada, Australia, Japan

Cover: Foto ©Andreas Hilbeck / pixelio.de

More available books at **www.hansebooks.com**

BY AND BY.

An Historical Romance of the Future.

BY

EDWARD MAITLAND,

AUTHOR OF

"THE PILGRIM AND THE SHRINE," "HIGHER LAW," ETC.

"In those days shall——"
Ancient Prophecy.

IN THREE VOLUMES.

VOL. III. . .

LONDON:

RICHARD BENTLEY AND SON.

1873.

BY AND BY.

CHAPTER V.

THE vast works in progress in Soudan were exciting widespread attention and interest. Already had the Empire of the African Plateau made such an advance in importance and civilisation, that the probability of its early admission into the Confederacy of Nations was everywhere allowed. Such promotion as this was beyond the dreams of the previous sovereigns of Soudan, and the people were elated beyond measure at the prospect. Not only would such admission be a recognition of their claim to rank among civilised communities, but it would be worth a large percentage in

the money-markets of the world. Could Criss
and the Emperor secure this admission, they
would gain for the country an advantage
greater than that which they had in vain
sought from the Stock Exchange of Jerusalem. Even the people of Soudan now
saw the impolicy of their once proposed re-
pudiation.

Of course, as in every partially civilised
community, there were people whose vested
interests were opposed to the new state of
things, and who thought that their interests
ought to be paramount. In order to be recognised as sufficiently civilised to be admitted to the Confederation, it is indispensable that the candidate-nation prove itself
amenable to the ordinary processes of reason
in its various public departments, and that all
parts of its system be consistent with each
other. Thus, there is no chance of entrance
for a people whose institutions rest avowedly
on a basis of mere tradition. For the civilised
world has learnt by experience that experience is the only trustworthy basis of stability,
whether in public policy, religion, or morals.
For instance, to have a national church, or

not to have one, is in the view of the Elective Council of the Confederation a matter of
indifference ; but the existence of a Church,
or of any other public institution, resting
avowedly upon a traditional or dogmatic
basis, is fatal to the chances of the claimant.

Not only was Soudan at this time in-
admissible on the ground of its having a
national church of this kind, but it carried
its defiance of logic and consistency to so
incredible an extent as to maintain two national institutions, directly opposed to each
other, both in principle and in practice. For,
in its National schools, which were derived
from the Mahommedan period of the country,
it gave an education which consisted, as with
us, in the cultivation of the intelligence and
moral sense of the children ; while, in its
National Church, which dated from the change
to Christianity, and owed its existence to
the personal influence of the royal house of
Abyssinia, it denounced the human mind and
conscience as delusive and pernicious, and
claimed the assent of all to a theory of the
Universe and system of theology which failed
utterly to commend themselves to those

faculties. Thus, at this time Soudan was in the category of what the Council is accustomed to schedule as *Lunatic* Nations, inasmuch as it had no settled principle of action, and pulled down on one side all that it upheld on the other.

Enlightened by Criss, it was now the Emperor's ambition to remove this stigma, by placing the national preacher in accord with the national schoolmaster. His pride revolted against the notion of his being regarded by the highest civilisations in the world as but a Sovereign of fools. And pride, Criss found to his regret, was the leading motive to which his cousin was amenable. Next to pride, and obstinacy on behalf of his own way, came the sentiment of affection for his cousin. In the conflict between these feelings, Criss not unfrequently found himself compelled to appeal to his pride in order to turn the balance in the desired direction. It was by acting on this motive that the native combativeness of the young ruler had finally been enlisted on behalf of radical reform. Having once resolved to win the approbation of Europe by abolishing the absurd incongruity between the preacher and the teacher, the very hostility of the vested interests, which fattened upon the existing system, served to strengthen his purpose. To this end he listened eagerly to all that his cousin had to say on the subject.

Educated under the impression that the Priest was the natural and indispensable sustainer of the Crown, he was surprised, as well as delighted, at the array of incontrovertible evidences whereby Criss showed him that the Priest has never supported anything save for his own ends, and that the whole history of priesthoods, of whatever age, country, or religion, shows those bodies to be, by their very nature and constitution, utterly and irredeemably selfish, making their own aggrandisement, individually or corporately, the one object and aim of their policy. Criss wound up his homily on this occasion by saying,—

" Ah, if they had only striven for man's regeneration here, with but a fraction of the persistency with which they have invoked the hereafter ! But, as it is, there is no cruel or degrading superstition, from the belief in demons and witchcraft, to that in human sacrifices and eternal torture, that they have not fostered and turned to their own account. I repeat but a trite historical truth when I say that the priest, as priest, is both enemy of man and libeller of God; and that the throne which has such a foundation can only be that of a tyrant. This, so far as the people are concerned. With regard to the ruler, it is the least secure of bases. For the very theory of Ecclesiasticism is subversive of all civil government. In order to be the ruler and redeemer of your people, you must begin by effacing every vestige of sacerdotalism from the public institutions of the country. Of course, privately, people may hold and teach what they please. But the State can recognise and support only what is consistent with the equal liberty of all and its own supremacy; and no ecclesiastical system is that."

"But my own throne," interrupted the Emperor, "what becomes then of my divine right? They have always upheld that."

"Divine right," replied Criss, "is but a dogma. Real right has no need of dogma. If use and experience do not justify your throne's existence, no authority of dogma will do so, and the sooner it is subverted the better. But the fact is, where a church is supreme, neither sovereign nor people can be free. It is never content until it has subjugated the souls and bodies of men. Such is the nature, avowed or concealed, of all priesthoods."

" When you urge me to take up a position in antagonism to the priesthood, do you not mean the church ?"

" That is the very confusion that nearly cost England her own church. No, the priest is but an official of the church, and like any other official, is apt to forget that he exists, not for his own benefit, but as servant of the whole body. Keep the official under as strict control as may be necessary to secure the efficiency of his department. But the department itself, that is the church, must neither be destroyed nor cast adrift from the State. In the first place, it has a vitality that makes its destruction impossible, for it has its roots originally in the aspirations of human nature towards a higher life than that of the field, the factory, and the laboratory. In the

second place, if cast adrift from the temper-
ing influences of the State and the lay power,
it will grow up in the hands of its officials to
be a very Upas to the State. A free church
in a free State is an impossibility, especially
where the church is possessed of overwhelm-
ing wealth, prestige, and power. You might
as well try to imagine a free army in a free
State. No, the State alone can make and
keep the church free from any servitude to
which it is really liable, namely, that which
arises from the dominion of dogma, or the
arrogance of an hierarchy. We have proved
all this long ago in England, so that your
task is a simple one. You have but to make
your church in reality what it is in name—
National. And this you can do only by re-
leasing it from all limitations upon opinion
and expression, and allowing any man of
proved education and capacity to minister in
it, unfettered by tradition. Your church
will then be the fitting crown to your schools
and universities ; and the whole national part
of the educational apparatus of the country
will be of a piece throughout, for it will have
its bases in the human mind and conscience,

and its apex in the sky, with God and idealised Humanity."

"But what," asked the Emperor, "am I to reply to my clergy when they make reproachful appeal to me to know what will become of the truths of religion when their teaching is no longer compulsory?"

"Say," replied Criss, "precisely what becomes of the truths of science when unshackled by foregone conclusions. They will have free course and be glorified. Religion will cease to be a worship of the dead, and become the apotheosis of the living, the actual. Whatever is good and useful and necessary, can be shown to be so by evidence, without aid from dogma. We want no authority beyond that of evidence to make us hold that the earth goes round the sun. Indeed, until men abandoned authoritative tradition on that subject, they believed a falsehood. No, the bases of that which is good, useful, and true, must be perpetually verifiable, otherwise it ceases to be good, useful, and true."

"But surely a national church implies a national religion?"

" By no means. There can be no such thing as a national religion, any more than a national set of truths or facts, or a national system of medicine, science, or art. There may, and should be, a national institution for educating the faculties which are devoted to such ends, and for extending such education, as only a national institution can do, to every corner of the land ; but the phrase ' national religion' involves as great an absurdity as the phrase ' national God.'"

" My clergy will have a good deal to un-learn," remarked the Emperor.

" So had ours. Yet they did it. But those who care for Humanity and Truth will not mind that."

The Emperor shook his head.

" Vested interests are strong and selfish," he said. " I can do a good deal to make it worth their while, but I shall have a nest of hornets about me."

CHAPTER VI.

T was mainly the activity of the "nest of hornets" alluded to by the Emperor, that made Criss's presence in Soudan indispensable. The physical curse of the country might be dealt with by deputy. Its moral curse must be dealt with in person. The superstition of its people rendered the prolonged absence of their sovereign's good genius, as Criss was popularly called, a hindrance to the designs in progress for their own benefit. The clergy, seeing their cherished system of thought, or rather no thought, menaced, denounced the physical improvements, commenced or projected, as constituting an impious interference with the Divine Will. Such a notion could

be met only by the diffusion of a knowledge
of sound reasoning. In conjunction with
some of the more advanced citizens, Criss set
to work to found a propagandist agency for
this purpose. Taking for its motto, *Free
Enquiry and Free Expression*, this institution
had for its function the publication and
distribution in myriads of short pithy papers,
exposing the absurdities of the popular super-
stitions. I happen to have the originals of
some of these papers by me, in Criss's own
handwriting. It may be not amiss to repro-
duce one or two of them here, if only to
illustrate the mental condition of a people
placed by the Confederate Council in the
schedule of Lunacy. The following seems
to have been levelled at the objection just
referred to as raised by the priests :—

"THE DIVINE WILL.
"According to the priests of Soudan, a
will that can be thwarted by man. According
to common sense and the dictionaries, the
Supreme Will. People of Soudan, require
of your priests that they be careful of their
definitions."

Another, also in his own hand, was in
answer to the reproach of Atheism brought
against the new school.   It ran thus :—

" PEOPLE OF SOUDAN.
" Be not frightened by names.   There is
no Atheist, save he who disbelieves in cause
and effect.   To believe in a cause of all
things, is to believe in a God.   Respecting
the nature of that cause, it is not only lawful
but necessary to differ until determined by
positive evidence derived from a due comprehension of its effects, that is, of Nature.
The real Atheists now-a-days are those who
would banish God from the living present to
a dead past."

And this also :—

" SCIENCE ; WHAT IS IT ?
" Sound knowledge, obtained by accurate
observation of carefully ascertained facts.
To reject the scientific method for any other,
is to reject fact for fancy, truth for falsehood."

Hunting up the records of our own country at a corresponding period of its history, Criss founded also an agency called, *The Church of Soudan Nationalisation Society*, in exact imitation of the famous organisation which played so important a part in promoting the Emancipation. In the prospectus which he wrote for the chief organ of this society, a high-class weekly, also named after its British prototype, Criss showed the Soudanese how alone they could emulate the example of the England they so greatly admired. " The course of all modern civilisation," he said in this manifesto, " is from a point at which human life is entirely subordinated to tradition and authority derived from a remote past, to a point at which the sole appeal is to the cultivated intelligence and moral sense of the living generations of men. Desirous of traversing that course, as England has done, let us not be discouraged by its difficulties. It is true it took England several centuries to make the journey. But then she had to do it by herself and in faith, for she had no example before her to encourage her. It is not so

with us. The whole civilised world, backed |
by the experience of the ages, is on our side.
The *Reformation*, the name whereby this
course was known, released England from
the domination of that ancient enemy of
human freedom, Rome, some four hundred
years before she detached herself from the
domination of Dogma, which was of Rome.
This achieved, the glorious *Reformation*
bloomed and bore its fruit in the more
glorious *Emancipation*. The path has been
shown us ; we need not be long in traversing
it."

The clergy of Soudan, in their alarm at
the new movement, sought to strike at its
promoters through the neighbouring peoples.
Divining that the Emperor's design of rege-
nerating the Plateau involved the redemption
of the Sahara, they set to work to stir up
the desert tribes, the people of Fezzan, and
those bordering on the Mediterranean,
by asserting that it was the intention of the
Emperor, under European influence, to destroy their commerce and power by bringing
in the sea to drown them out. The trigono-
metrical survey they denounced as an inven-

tion of the Evil one, and liable to be visited with a retribution such as that which had followed the census of David; and Africa was still so dark a continent, intellectually, despite its superabundance of physical sunlight, as to make the idea terrible to the multitude.

Such was the position when Criss tore himself from Nannie, whom he had in vain endeavoured to interest in his work, to make his first post-nuptial visit to Africa. Occupied as he had been with his domestic affairs, and inexpressibly shocked and bewildered by the unexpected development in his wife of a passion which he could neither comprehend nor moderate, he yet had not allowed himself to be idle, and in much of his work he found Avenil an admirable helper. Not in his missionary zeal for the direct spiritual enlightenment of the Soudanese:—there Avenil had no sympathy, ascribing it to the Semitic element in his blood. But he gladly encouraged his Teutonic tendencies, and directed all the consultations of his engineers and draughtsmen. One portion of Criss's

work consisted in the construction of picto-
rial representations of the Africa of the
future—Africa as he hoped to make it—no
longer blasted and cursed by its own sunshine, but with its Sahara turned into a
smiling garden, or a summer sea. Criss's pic-
torial designs had already done wonders, and
it now remained only to conciliate the dwellers
in the Oases, the most superstitiously attached
of mortals to their green homes. Sooner, it
was said, would an Arab give up his hope of
heaven, than part with his beloved oasis, the
birth-place, dwelling-place, and final resting-
place, alike of himself and his ancestors. The
provinces on the coast hailed with delight a
scheme that, if successful, would reverse the
geological decree which attached them to
Africa, and restore them virtually to Europe,
as well as relieve them of the miseries inflicted by the desert blasts ; and which, even
if unsuccessful, would do them no harm. All
along the coast, from the low-lying Gulf of
Cabes, from the Gulf of Sidra, and almost
up to Egypt itself, came offers of territory
through which to cut the canals by which the
Mediterranean was to flow into the desert,

and a communication maintained between the
two seas. Almost up to Egypt. There the
tone was different. Egypt would not hear of
such an experiment. She not only placed
her veto upon it, but stirred up the Arabs
inhabiting the Libyan Oases, the most depressed portions of the Sahara, to resist it
with all their might. This action of Egypt
was accounted by the Emperor of Soudan
an additional cause for the enmity he cherished in his heart, but kept secret from his
cousin.

As the vast design got wind, all Europe
and Asia Minor became interested in it, and
the students of science eagerly fought over
their conflicting theories respecting the pro-
babilities and consequences of success. The
Geologists, whatever their theories on these
points, were to a man enthusiastic on behalf
of the experiment. They even afforded
useful aid to the project by exhibiting to the
astonished Arabs the fossil remains of fishes,
which they found in the Sahara, proving that
it was the sea-bed of an evaporated ocean of
the Tertiary period, and therefore possibly

designed by Providence again to become a
sea. The Geologists did service also by suggesting the probability of there being under-
ground reservoirs of fresh water permeating
the limestone bed of the Sahara. Where
else could all the water which annually inun-
dated the plateau, go to ? And if this was
the case, doubtless it was from this inexhaust-
ible source that the Oases were fed. What
then would be easier or better than to enlarge the apertures and let more of this
water flow through to the surface ? Indeed,
it might thus be a fresh instead of a salt sea,
that the Sahara would become.

Avenil and Criss discussed this together.
They came to the conclusion that it was
probable, that on making an extensive verti-
cal boring into the Sahara, the first flow of
water would be fresh, and might continue so
for some time. But that, ultimately, the sea
which was at present kept out by the fresh
water, would fill in the limestone cavities,
and flow through into the Sahara. Should
it only come through in sufficient quantity
to counteract the loss by evaporation, the
problem of turning the desert into a sea

would be solved, and that without cutting a canal.

They communicated the notion to the Emperor, who was hereditary chief over a small oasis, which lay close below the Plateau, considerably to the east of Lake Tchad, and therefore far towards Egypt. He caught at the suggestion, and having purchased the rights of all the dwellers on the oasis, and removed them to an estate at a distance, he sent a strong force of labourers, with powerful excavating machinery, and set them to work to bore for water on a large scale.

The result of the experiment was satisfactory beyond expectation, considering that the spot selected was by no means one of the lowest parts of the desert. The water, thus far perfectly fresh and pure, came through in such abundance, that the whole oasis was flooded, and continued to be so, as well as the surrounding desert for a considerable distance, until the sands and the sun prevailed to prevent its further spread.

Students of science, other than geologists, concerned themselves with the doings in the

Sahara. These were the Meteorologists; especially the Meteorologists of Switzerland. " In the glacial period," said they, " Switzerland was an iceberg. From the summit of the Alps to beyond the Jura, it was buried beneath the chilling pressure of an enormous mass of ice, bearing on its surface giant rocks. The great desert of the Sahara was still overflowed by the waves of the sea ; its burning sands not yet exposed so as to produce that glowing wind which, now-a-days, after traversing the Mediterranean, melts away the winter snows on the Alps, as if by magic, and converts Switzerland into a blooming country."

" To restore the sea to the Sahara," exclaimed the savants, " is to bring back the glacial period to Switzerland. It is to ruin the climate of Europe."

The question was an immense one. With the climate of Europe would go the civilisation of Europe. The world would have existed in vain. Every scientific coterie on the face of the globe was absorbed in the problem. It was one of the " long results of time," that International politics became a

question of Meteorology. This was something gained in the long and weary pilgrim-
age of Humanity. But what would Alex-
ander, Julius Cæsar, or Napoleon Bonaparte
have thought of such a controversy between
nations ?

Criss, as was his wont, had recourse to
Avenil. Avenil had enjoyed the discussion,
but held the fears to be groundless. In the
first place, said he, the sea will be a very
shallow and a very warm one, and the bed
has been raised so high, that probably one
half will not be submerged. Of this, however, we shall be better able to judge when
the survey is completed. But there is another reason. The greatest cold of Europe
comes with the North-east Trades from Polar
Russia. These winds are aggravated, if not
entirely caused, by the heat of North Africa.
Cool Africa, and you mitigate, not increase,
the rigour of the climate of Europe.

The states bordering on the Sahara took
another view of the question. " What," they
asked, " is the climate of Europe to us ? We
have a right to escape from being roasted in
our own country, if we can."

The determination taken by Criss was to make the experiment, as an experiment to be abandoned in the event of success proving pernicious. There would be no difficulty about this.

In spite of the opposition of Egypt—an opposition offered on purely selfish grounds— Criss succeeded in purchasing the most eligible portion of the country bordering on the Mediterranean for his purpose. It lay between Tripoli and Egypt, and contained a region depressed nearly two hundred feet below the sea.

The spot where the excavation was to commence was from one to two hundred miles inland. Here, and at numerous points along the route, was collected an army of labourers, with excavating machinery of gigantic power, and a vast array of appliances for the task. The plan was to cut a deep broad channel in the solid limestone bed of the desert to the sea, maintaining the same depth throughout, so as to make way for an enormous body of water to enter at once. Thus only, it was held, would the loss by evaporation be supplied. Notwithstanding

the efforts brought to bear upon it, the works
would occupy several years.

To Criss's perplexity, the Emperor did
not enter so heartily into this portion of the
scheme. Taking a line of his own, he pretended that he disliked the idea of an open
junction with the Mediterranean, by which
hostile, and rival trading vessels would be
enabled to traverse the inland sea up to the
very borders of his country. He might be a
match, he said, for his African rivals, but
could not compete with the whole world.
Rather than have an open channel, he would
prefer to bring the sea in through a series of
enormous siphons. It was only that he
might conciliate the nations of the Confederacy, and secure his own admission into it,
that he would consent to Criss's scheme.

Criss felt that the Emperor had not given
the real grounds of his objection, and urged
him further.

The Emperor then said that he was convinced that no single channel could supply
the Sahara, and that he thought that tunnels
might be driven with advantage, and at far
less cost, into the sea at various points round

the coast, so as to make sure of the water
reaching any isolated portion of the low lands.
He proposed to attack in this way both the
Atlantic and the Red Sea. A tunnel through
the limestone ranges of Abyssinia would not
only bring in water from a greater height
than at any other point—for the earth's con-
figuration and motion, and the influence of
the winds and tides, were such as to keep the
Red Sea at a higher level than any other on
the African coast—but it would afford a cheap
and convenient mode of transit for heavy produce to an Abyssinian port. At any rate, he
had set his heart upon making the attempt,
and should do his best to carry out the latter
portion of the project at once, whilst Criss was
operating in the direction of the Mediterranean. He had already consulted with his
ministers, as well as with the savants and
imperial engineers, and their report had
secured the co-operation of the principal
capitalists of Soudan. He concluded by
challenging Criss to a race, to see who would
first bring the water in, himself from the Red
Sea, or Criss from the Mediterranean.

CHAPTER VII.

CRISS'S life was indeed a full one. While engaged in the regeneration, moral and physical, of a continent, his own heart was perpetually torn asunder between the two characters alternately enacted by his wife Nannie.

Two characters, different as those of two women. The one, so ineffably lovely and loving, winning and kind, in the ecstasy of her ardent nature abandoning herself wholly to her love, and in the perfection of her adaptation making Criss feel indeed that if ever woman was made for man, Nannie must have been made expressly for him.

The other, the result of abandonment, not to love, but to feelings which converted love itself into a curse. Nannie knew and felt

that Criss loved her wholly, solely, and truly ;
but, unaccustomed as she had ever been to
exercise the slightest control over herself, she
now gave herself up to the dominion of her
fancies, until, although knowing, and in her
calmer moments admitting them to be but
fancies, they became for her more than all
facts ; more even than all convictions, which
to the female mind are too apt to be far more
than facts.

These fancies all took one shape. She
understood love only as a monopoly. Her
lover was unfaithful to her if he had friend-
ships, interests, thoughts, occupations, in which
she was not all in all. So far from her love
leading her to take an interest in whatever
interested him,. it led her at first to exhibit
indifference to, and then vehemently abuse,
every object, event, or person unconnected
with her, that he chanced to mention. Slowly
and sadly he found himself driven to a resolution never to allude in her presence to any
subject whatever, save herself. Even his
own life-long friends were not spared, though
she was never tired of vaunting her own
early associations.

Criss alone saw her under the influence of this side of her character. In society her brightness and vivacity won immense admiration, and admiration was a thing which she loved too dearly to forfeit by an exhibition of ill-temper. While the self-control thus manifested abroad led Criss to hope the best for her sanity, he found no consolation in ascribing her outrageous conduct at home to a deliberate disregard for him and his happiness. One of the traits which struck him as most curious, was the utter indifference she showed to her promises of reformation, and this only a little while after she had uttered them with such exhibition of deep repentant sorrow as to win his forgiveness, and make him hope that this was really the last time.

But though none of his friends as yet were cognisant of his domestic history, they could not fail to remark that he withdrew more and more from their society, and that when he did appear, he had little of the serenity and cheerfulness which had been wont to characterise him. Criss had a good and tried friend in his neighbour, Dr. Markwell, a physician of high repute, and married to a medical lady

whom also he highly esteemed. But it was
only by stealth and rarely that he ventured
to consult them. He feared to excite Nannie's
suspiciousness and jealousy against even her
physician. For the doctor to be able to
influence her, he must retain her confidence.
It was thus that when they met in Nannie's
presence, he affected to give but a qualified
assent to whatever Criss said.

An astute investigator of the maladies of
mankind, Dr. Markwell, while assuring Nannie that it lay with herself to determine her
own fate, whether for weal or woe, inasmuch
as it is to a very great extent in the power of
an individual to promote or resist insanity ;—
while, too, he gave Criss hope that her mind
might be beneficially distracted from its fatal
preoccupation by the advent of offspring, yet
in his own mind feared the worst.

He did not, however, consider it his duty
altogether to conceal from Criss the nature of
his fears. Having had much experience in
prisons, and observed the effect produced
upon the female constitution by the absence
of a habit of control whether by self or by
another, he told Criss how that when once a

young woman has discovered her power to produce an hysterical paroxysm at will, she is liable to exercise it for her own gratification, without regard to the distress she may cause to others ; and that, the habit once induced, her own mental and moral nature is at the mercy of it, and madness in one of its many forms frequently supervenes.

" It was precisely such a condition of mental intoxication," he continued, " that in former times it was the ambition of the religious fanatics of various countries to produce in themselves or their converts. From the ecstatic utterances of a pagan sibyl, to the hysterical convulsions of a Christian revivalist, the condition and its character were the same. It was only when the law sternly forbade fanatics, who mistook their own ignorance of physiology for inspiration, to propagate madness—as it before had forbidden pretended sorcerers to trade upon credulity— that our own country was finally freed from the disgrace of such scenes. Woman's nature, however, remains the same. Its emotional side requires to be counterbalanced by the most carefully developed reason,—reason of

her own, or reason of man. If it is not good
for man to be alone, ten thousand times less
is it good for woman to be alone, or uncontrolled by a strong hand. There are cases in
which kindness to her is but unkindness ;—in
which the sense of duty needs the stimulus of
fear to keep it up to the mark."

This last observation reminded Criss of
Nannie's strange utterance respecting her sister, and the regime of physical correction on
which she insisted. He mentioned it, and, in
reply to the doctor's commentary, said, smiling
sadly,—

" Well, doctor, if my wife does not mend
until I beat her, I fear she must continue
to behave ill until the end of the chapter."

" Ah, that is because you have a theory
which bears no relation to experience," returned the doctor. " Forgive me for saying
it, but it seems to me self-evident that if, in
order to spare your own feelings, or in deference to a supposed principle, you abstain from
the course best calculated to benefit her, you
are acting selfishly instead of benevolently,
and following dogma rather than experience."

"How like a speech of Avenil's!" exclaimed Criss.

"You must understand," continued the doctor, "that there is among women of undeveloped intellect, when they have done wrong, a certain craving for chastisement, growing out of a rudimentary sense of justice. When a man sees that he has made a mistake, he manifests his repentance by resolving not to repeat it. Not so a woman. Half the power of priests over women in old times con sisted in their habit of hearing their confessions and imposing penances. The husband is the successor of the priest. He must listen sympathetically to his wife's confessions, and assign the appropriate penance, or inflict the appropriate penalty. The less she is able to govern herself, the more he must govern her. For lack of the husband, it should be the doctor. But I really consider that the man who compels himself to be harsh to the woman he loves, solely for her own good, performs the loftiest act of self-renunciation possible to a finite being. Of course, I do not prescribe extreme measures at the very outset. I mean only that, kindness having

failed, the treatment must be changed for one
of apparent harshness. Your wife, for instance, declares that she goes wild with
misery the moment you go out of her sight.
Suppose, then, that you exercise her in the
art of self-control by allowancing her, and
making the amount of time you pass with her
dependent on her success in repressing that
feeling. She might be induced to cut a
paroxysm short if she knew that her indul-
gence in it would deprive her of your society
for the next four-and-twenty hours or more."

" Are the constitutional differences between
the sexes so radical and extreme ?" asked
Criss.

" They are, indeed. I do not mean to say,
however, that man is never as foolish and
irrational as ever woman can be. It is possible that at times he can beat her in that, as
in most other things ; but when a man is
so, it is in spite of his sex, and when a woman
is so, it is owing to her sex——"

" All the more cause for extra tenderness
and patience, then," interrupted Criss ; but
the doctor went on without heeding.

" The history of woman's efforts to reverse

Nature's decree is one of the most curious in
the world. Ridiculed by Aristophanes, there
are not wanting some to return to the charge
even now, that is, in less advanced countries.
Here, our women have long ago learnt to
recognise the fact, and to make the best of it
without striving to alter it. But it was only
after the men had consented to their making
the attempt, and so demonstrating their limitations by experience, that they settled finally
into their own place. I confess, as a medical
man, I cannot see how any woman that was
wife and mother, ever so mistook her own
nature."

In one respect Criss followed the doctor's
advice. He ceased to go through the form
of consulting or affecting to please Nannie, in
any arrangements he was obliged to make.
He simply said, " Nannie, I shall be absent
for so many hours, or days." And when she
broke into angry reproaches,—" Nannie, you
are taking the very means to lengthen my
absence. I have not now for the first time to
assure you that the more you keep this tem-
per under, the more I shall be with you, and
the happier we shall be."

The birth of a child served to restore hope
and happiness to both husband and wife.
Criss had looked forward to this event with
intense eagerness, believing that all depended
upon it. With such a *fact* ever present to
her, Nannie surely would not now indulge in
fancies.

It was a girl—as Nannie ardently desired—but she was not quite reconciled to
her being called Zöe, after the mother whom
Criss had never seen. It made her jealous
of that mother.

Nannie had borne Criss's absence in Africa
far better than the scene at his departure had
suffered him to hope. Doctress Markwell
had read her rightly when she said to Criss,

" Take courage. Without you at hand to
be distressed at her fancies, she will not care
to indulge them. She has not reached the
stage at which she would take delight in tor-
menting herself without your being a sharer.
I hope she never may."

It took some time after his return for the
old fancies to show themselves. And then
Zöe arrived opportunely to allay Criss's re-
viving anxiety. With the child came all joy

and forgetfulness of past troubles—such utter forgetfulness on Nannie's part of her own extravagances of behaviour, as to kindle in Criss a new apprehension. But, refusing to entertain it, he gave himself up to the delights of the situation. This new idea was that Nannie, though supremely endowed as a woman, was devoid of that essential element of humanity recognised by him under the name of *Soul.* He could not otherwise account for her utter lack of self-consciousness or sense of responsibility for past conduct. The child bid fair to resemble its mother, save in one respect. It had its father's eyes. Surely, then, his Zöe at least would have a soul !

Nannie made an admirable mother, as she had always boasted she would. The pride she took in her infant, and consequent eagerness to exhibit it to visitors, led Criss to hope that she had got the better of another weak-ness—namely, her aversion to all society save that of himself.

In short, so conformable was Nannie to all requirements of propriety, health, and motherly perfection, that Criss began to think that the painful scenes of altercation and violence which had made him so wretched must have been but an ugly dream, or at worst but a spasmodic throe of nature over the production of a first-born.

The doctor owned himself surprised at the completeness of the change; but he was too well habituated to note the distinction between the functional and the radical to express himself sanguinely about its permanence. He knew the instinctive liability of young mothers to use their infants as a weapon of coercion against the timid and doting father. " Thwart and irritate me, and your child suffers in consequence," was a dictum he had too often known uttered or signified in pursuance of an utterly irrational demand.

Fully impressed with the belief that Nannie's malady had resulted from physical causes, Criss trusted, by keeping her beyond the influence of those causes, to prevent a recurrence of the malady. He was so happy now in his own and Nannie's happiness in the society of their infant, that it seemed to

him an act of wantonness to do aught that
might endanger its continuance.

Nannie thought differently. She longed
to multiply her triumphs in the newly-won
domain of maternity, and scoffed at the notion of her being less robust in constitution
than any other of her sex. She even ascribed
to coldness and indifference to her pleasure
the tender, self-denying care with which Criss
sought to shield her from aught that might
excite and injure her. In short, she manifested all the symptoms of a relapse into the
old sad state.

Entreating her to be calm, he sought, by
pleading the danger to their child and their
own happiness, to win her consent to a regime
that might prevent a return of the illness
which had already caused them so much
misery.

" Illness ! What illness ?" she asked.

" You know all that we went through together, darling, before our little one was
born," he said. " Well, that was entirely the
result of your delicacy of constitution. I
love this present happiness too well to risk a
return of that evil time."

" I don't know what you are talking about,"
she returned. " I was not ill. I was only
jealous, as I had a right to be ; and as I shall
be again unless—unless— Oh, dear Criss !
you must not say or imagine such things.
Think what will become of baby, if you
upset me, and make me ill with such talk !"

" Ah, if you knew how terrible has been
my anxiety, you would not urge me to act
against my better judgment."

" A fig for better judgment ! You mean
that you no longer care for me, or you would
let me have my own way in everything."

" Why, Nannie, what an actress you would
have made. You said and looked that speech
to perfection."

" I was not acting ; I meant it."

" Well, do not excite yourself, I entreat.
Trust to me to do what is best. My precious wife does not know everything that is
in the world, or even in her own constitution,
though I acknowledge her to be a wonderful
little woman. Some day, perhaps, when you
are quite, quite strong, and I have talked to
Doctor, and you to Doctress Markwell, we
can do numbers of things which would be

dangerous to you now. I love my Nannie far too well to run the chance of losing her, especially by an imprudence that can so easily be avoided."

"I know best, without consulting any doctors," she exclaimed. "I believe you are in league with them against me. They always say just what you want them to." And she broke into a fit of that hysterical sobbing of which Criss had so lively a recollection and dread.

He had learnt by experience that to attempt to coax her out of those fits by soft speeches, was as great a mistake as to seek to appease a spoilt child by giving it everything it cries for. Resuming, therefore, once again the stern tone and aspect which he had hoped were done with for ever, he said,—

"Very well, Nannie; if you can act thus now, it is ample proof that you are unfit for the liberty which you desire. I intend to regard your power of self-control as my index to the state of your health."

"I care for nothing of that sort! I am master now! Look here," she cried excitedly, and holding the child aloft in her arms ; "do

you see this ? This makes me master ; and
I mean to have my own way in everything,
or you and your child will be the worse."
And she glared almost maniacally upon him.

By a movement too sudden for her to
thwart, he snatched the child from her, for
he really feared for its safety. Then sum-
moning the nurse, he said,—

" Take the child into your own room, and
do your best with it there until the arrival of
the wet-nurse, who will be here to-morrow."
And he placed his arm around Nannie, to
keep her from rushing after the child.

After two or three vain attempts to escape,
she sank back into her sofa, moaning and
sobbing.

When they were alone he said,—

" Now take this sedative, and sleep yourself good again. And whenever you find
the naughty fit coming over you, remember
that even with the child, I am still master,
and intend to be so."

" I want my child," she moaned, piteously.

" Not because you love it," returned Criss.

" I do love it. It is the only thing I love,
now that I hate you."

"And it is because you love it, that you insist upon making yourself so ill that you could not nurse it without making it ill likewise ? Ah, Nannie, dear, you have yet to learn what real love means—even the love of a mother for her infant."

He prevailed at last, and she took the draught, declaring that she only did so on condition that she should have the child back in the morning. He [did not accede to the condition, but the night's rest took such good effect, that the doctor found no reason to forbid the child returning to her. He complimented Criss on the wet-nurse, saying it was a master-stroke, and would doubtless bear repetition, if necessary. As for Nannie, she was so terrified by it, that several days passed before she again ventured to assert her own will in opposition to Criss's. Her first utterance to him in respect to the occurrence of that night was,—

"It ought to show you how perfect a woman you have got for a wife, when I gave up my own will for the sake of my child."

Criss was not aware that she had done so, but thought it was rather for her own sake;

but he did not care to contradict her on a mere matter of opinion. And happiness was restored, for she forbore for the present to renew the controversy which had caused the interruption to it.

CHAPTER VIII.

CRISS endeavoured to compensate for his absence from the scene of his operations in Africa, by the constancy of his intercourse by telegraph. One room in his house was set apart as his study, and one part of this study was occupied by a telegraphic apparatus, and wires which communicated with all the principal centres of his interest. Thus, he had his own private wire to Avenil's study : another to Bertie's cottage : one to the Triangle : another to his banker's; and he had also engaged the exclusive use of one to Africa, with branches to Bornou and the works in the desert. In this room he sat, and conducted his various correspondence,

arrangements being made to give notice, by
means of signals in other parts of the house,
when his attention was required in the telegraph room. As his library also was here,
and the walls were covered with maps and
drawings, as the shelves with books, Criss, as
he sat there, was surrounded by the whole
world of the past and present, while he
busied himself about that of the future.

In his care for the remote, whether in time
or in space, the near was not forgotten, and
poverty and sickness which, in spite of all
the advances made by civilisation, will still
occasionally thrust their ugly heads into view,
found in him an ever ready and sympathetic
alleviator. In the early days of his married
life, he had hoped to interest Nannie in some
of his local charities, but had been compelled
to give up the idea. She could scold people
for being bad managers, and by something
more direct than implication, praise herself;
but her sympathies seemed incapable of the
extension necessary to constitute charity. As
she could not with any advantage accompany
Criss on his rounds, and resented his absences, he had gradually withdrawn in a great

measure from making them, leaving his work to be done by deputy; an office gladly undertaken by the benevolent Bertie.

Of Criss's wealth, and the employment it gave him, Nannie had long been jealous; but now her jealousy extended itself to his home occupations, which he carried on in his study. Not that she was excluded from this apartment, for Criss delighted in being able to glance from his work to her, as she sat on the soft carpet playing with the little Zöe; but, unluckily, it occurred to her one day, that he could not be thinking entirely of her while occupied about other matters.

" Please explain, Nannie," he said one day, on her persisting in reproaching him for his engrossment. · " Please explain exactly what it is you wish of me; for I am really at my wits' end to understand. Is it that you wish me to cease to be a man, engaged in work worthy of a man, and to become a woman, with thoughts for nothing but love ?"

" Yes," said Nannie, stoutly. " I want you to think of nothing but me—and little Zöe ; but not much of her, or you will make me jealous of my own child."

" Nannie, there was once a poet who wrote to his lady-love,—

> "' I could not love thee, dear, so much,
> Loved I not honour more.'

What do you think of the sentiment ?"

" I should have been jealous of 'honour.' "

" You mean *for* honour, for *his* honour."

" No, I don't. I mean what I said."

" There was another poet, who described a wife of whom her husband was so fond, that he could not tear himself from her side to fulfil the duties to which he was in honour bound. One night he woke from his sleep to find her sitting up and murmuring, as she reflected over the career and character he was losing for her sake,—

> " ' Ah me, I fear me I am no true wife.'

Would you like to be regarded by your husband as being ' no true wife,' when you seek to detain him from his duties ?"

" I should have liked that man," she said. " He loved his wife as a woman ought to be loved. He would have owned me to be true woman, if not true wife."

At this moment Criss's attention was called off by the sounding of the telegraph signal. Before he was aware what she was about, Nannie had snatched a heavy ruler from the table, and rushing to the apparatus, with a tremendous blow smashed it to pieces.

"There!" she exclaimed, to Criss. "You may think yourself fortunate it was not your head. It may come to that yet, for your treatment of me."

Criss had learnt the futility of bandying words with her when such a mood was on her. Fearing for the safety of the child, he placed himself between her and it, and summoned the nurse.

"Go at once to Dr. Markwell's," he said, when the nurse arrived, "and give my compliments to him and Mrs. Markwell, and say that I shall be much obliged by their allowing you and the child to stay there until some other arrangement can be made."

"And when am I to see it again?" asked Nannie, as the nurse disappeared, and Criss closed the door after her.

"Well," he said, with simulated indifference, "I should think a week or two will probably see you over this attack. It will be time enough to think about it then."

And he set himself to examine the mischief done to his apparatus.

" I shall go after my child," exclaimed Nannie, darting towards the door.

" You cannot leave the room. I fastened the door as I let the nurse out. Your violence suggested the precaution."

" I won't stay in the house to be outraged."

" No one wishes you to do so. But you do not leave it until you are in your right mind, and then desire to do so. It depends entirely on yourself when that may be."

" Do you consider me mad, then ?"

" You force me to wish sometimes that I did."

" To wish that I was mad ?"

" Yes ; I should then be able to account for your behaviour. I would rather have you mad than bad ; heart-broken as it would make me."

" What does the doctor say about me ?"

" He thinks that whatever you may be at

present, you are endeavouring to drive yourself into insanity."

" Is that Mrs. Markwell's opinion, too ?"

" She says you are no more mad than
she is."

" What, then, does she ascribe my conduct
to ?"

" Uncontrolled wilfulness and inordinate
vanity."

" Nothing else ?"

" Not that I know of."

" She is right, so far ; but she omits the
principal cause."

" May I know it ?"

" You do know it. I have told you often."

" Tell me again."

" Love for you."

" Love for me makes you pain and distress
me by such conduct !"

" I can't help it."

" Nannie, answer truly. Do you try ?"

" I have no time, when my feelings move
me. You don't know what it is to have
feelings."

" I know what it is to have feelings for
others. You make me fear that yours are

only for yourself. Are you the happier
when you have given way to what you call
your feelings, and made me wretched, and
yourself ill, and ugly with passion, and driven
your child away—"

"Ugly! me ugly!" And she ran to a
mirror, and took a rapid look at herself; and
then, finding the survey satisfactory, she
rushed close up to Criss, and gazed with the
most exquisite, winning look imaginable, into
his face, and in a pleading tone asked,—

"Am I really ugly, Criss dear? I don't
think I am. Do you?" and putting her arms
round him she clasped him tightly to her.

"Is it then because you believe no man can
resist you, that you act in such a way?" he
enquired. "Believe me, Nannie, even you
may try your power too far. You have done
much to prove to me that even my patience
is limited."

"Why, what would you do?"

"Set you and myself free from a tie that
has become a bondage."

"Yes, I know that is what you want. But
I won't let you. I would murder her, and
you, and myself, too."

" Her ! your child ?"

" No, no, the woman you want to get free from me for."

" Oh, I see. You prefer that we should continue to be miserable together, than be happy apart."

" You don't deny, then, that there is a woman for whom you wish to give me up. I thought you had some motive for trying to kill me by your unkindness."

" Why should you give me credit for acting from motives, when you deny doing so your-self ?"

" Why should you care about other women when you have me ?"

" It seems to give you great pleasure to think that I do so."

" I think it because you can't help liking women. You like me too well not to like women."

" Oh ; and so you would behave better to me if I was less agreeable to you as a hus-band !"

" Yes ; it comes so natural to you to be nice with me, that I cannot help thinking you must have learnt it with others."

" I see. I shall have to imitate the example of the knight who always clad himself in his armour before caressing his wife, for fear she should find the process too agreeable."

" I know what men are. You don't deceive me when you pretend to be thinking only of my good. You will send me out of my mind by it, and then you will be sorry." And she began to cry.

" There is one thing, Nannie, that you have never yet got properly into your understanding :—that I took you to be, not my master, but my mistress. So long as you strive to be both, you shall be neither. That is positive and certain. You have but to choose."

" May I choose now ?"

" If you please."

" I—don't—want—to be your—master."

" You declare it faithfully, and will not try in future ?"

" Yes," she said, in a low penitent voice, gazing down while she spoke, and taking the measure of her own exquisite little foot, as, protruded from beneath her dress, it lay close along side of his.

He was silent awhile, pondering the propriety of giving her another trial, but feeling that she had not yet really repented of her recent outrageous behaviour.

Finding that he did not speak, she said, coaxingly,—-

" And you will let baby come back ?"

" Certainly, the moment you give me reason to feel sure you will continue to be good."

" I am good now."

" For how long ?"

" Until I am provoked again."

" That won't do. The child shall stay away altogether, rather than grow up to have its character ruined by witnessing an evil example set it by its mother."

"You will not rob my child of its mother !" she exclaimed wildly.

" On the contrary. I wish to save you to your child."

" Are my promises nothing?" she enquired.

" You are as well able to judge of that as I am. How have you kept them hitherto ?"

She hung her head, conscious that she had used words as counters, to be put aside as worthless so soon as her game was played.

" I shan't know what to do all day without my baby," she murmured,

" Yes, we shall miss it dreadfully," he remarked.

" You won't care," returned Nannie.

" Well, not so much as you, because I can go and see it occasionally."

" So can I," said Nannie. " I shall go now."

" That is quite out of the question."

" Why?"

" Because I have given orders to the contrary."

" What do you mean ?"

" Nannie, I had a most terrible shock one day, not long ago. I overheard, when out walking, some people talking about us. One said to the other, ' How is it one sees Mr. Carol about so little now?' I dread to tell you the answer; but it may do you good to know the impression you have produced in the neighbourhood."

" I am not afraid, what was it ?"

" ' Oh, poor fellow, he is afraid to leave his mad wife.' "

" I don't believe a word of it," said Nannie.

"It is nothing but a story you have made up to excuse yourself for going about without me."

"So far from that being the case, it is the greatest disappointment to me to find you object so to every thing I have to do, and every person I have to see, that I am compelled to leave you at home. But where do you imagine that I want to go without you?"

"I know."

"Will you not enlighten me? Of course, I should not have told you of that conversation if I considered you mad."

"It is no matter what you consider me. You like the society of other people. That is enough for me."

"But not in the same way that I like your society. Life has many kinds of pleasures and engrossments, besides love; which, by operating as distractions, serve to perpetuate and intensify love. Foremost among them are the charities and amenities of social inter-course, friendship, and intellectual converse. I take as much delight in these as ever; but I have withdrawn from them all, in the interests of your happiness."

" And quite right too. It only makes you despise me for my ignorance when you go among what you call intellectual people. As for friends, I don't see what you want with them, when you have got a wife."

" Nannie, I expected to find you untaught : but I did not expect to find you unteachable."

" Then you are disappointed in me ?"

" It is in your power to prevent my being so."

" If you loved me as you ought, you would think me perfect. But you can't, when you are always thinking of some other—some *intellectual*—woman." (She uttered the word with a sneering emphasis.) "Oh, you need not deny it. You won't convince me. I *know* it is true, because I dreamt it! Don't laugh at me! I won't be laughed at by you, oh, you cruel, cruel man!" she added, on seeing the smile evoked by her last speech.

" Why, Nannie, it is the greatest compliment one can pay to a comedian when he has uttered a good thing well, to laugh heartily. I shall make a note of that, ' I *know* it is true, because I dreamt it,' and get some dramatic friend to put it into a play. An actress who can say it exactly as you did, will be sure to bring the house down. But I really must bring this conversation to an end for the present, as I must go and see how poor Bertie is."

" Bertie ! what is the matter with him ?"

" He was taken very ill in the night, and had to send for a doctor."

" Why don't you telegraph instead of going ?"

" You have put it out of my power."

" How ?"

" I had already been conversing with him about himself by telegraph. It was the sounding of his signal that excited you to destroy the apparatus. By my not replying, he will be thinking that I have gone out, probably to see him."

" Is this true ?" she exclaimed.

" I know you have never understood my character," he replied; " but I did not think you had so utterly misunderstood it as to suppose me capable of falsehood."

" I know what I know," she said, with a menacing air that was anything but reassuring to Criss. And then with a sudden change of demeanour, added, " But Criss dear, I must go and nurse dear Bertie. I can be such a good nurse. You will be so proud of your little wife when you see her in a sick-room. Why did you not tell me at once, and then all this trouble would have been saved ?"

" I was about to tell you when it occurred, in the hope that you would make the proposal you have just made."

" Well then, come quick, and let us go to him at once. Shall I ring for the carriage ?"

" I will do that, while you are putting something on," replied Criss, utterly at a loss to find the key-note to a character that seemed determined to baffle him. He could liken Nannie only to a musical instrument, that is perfect in all respects, save for one note which obstinately refuses to be tuned into harmony, but so jars whenever and however it is touched, as to produce the most frightful discord. Only in Nannie's case, unhappily, the false note seemed to have the faculty of spontaneous utterance, so that it was impossible to avoid being tortured by it.

CHAPTER IX.

ERTIE'S illness was sharp, but by the evening the symptoms were so much alleviated, that there was no excuse for Criss and Nannie to remain with him through the night. In her conduct in the sick-room, Nannie had shown a tact and readiness which delighted Criss; and on their way home he spoke in such a way as to show her that he was pleased, but without implying that he was surprised. Nannie's demeanour during the drive each way, caused him some perplexity. On the way to Bertie's her lips were set, as if under the influence of alarm and apprehension. On her return she spoke only in monosyllables, as if his remarks interrupted a train of thoughts altogether unconnected with their recent experience. On reaching home she ran into the house without a word, and hurried upstairs, evidently longing to indulge her feelings by herself.

Anxiously watching, Criss heard a scream, which, however, did not sound to him like one of distress. In another moment Nannie had run down to him, with the baby in her arms, exclaiming triumphantly,—

"I have got her back! I have got her back!"

"Yes, so I see. Can you explain it?" he asked with a smile.

"No," she said, and her face fell, as if feeling less sure that she had cause for exultation.

"Bring baby into the study, and I will tell you."

"No, no, not in that room, I can't go in there. In here."

"Nannie, darling, I was so pleased by your readiness to go and nurse Bertie, that I sent for the child back to meet you on your return, as a reward."

For a moment Nannie looked as if she was on the point of bursting into tears. Then, with a manifest effort, she restrained

them, and after two or three fluctuations of
resolve, said, as if to herself,—

" No, I won't.   I won't be so weak.   He
shan't think he has conquered me.   Criss,
you were taken in.   It wasn't goodness a bit
that made me want to go to Bertie.   I didn't
believe your story about his being ill.   I
thought it was an excuse to go and see some
woman.   I determined to outwit you by
going with you.   And now I have got my
child back, without being good."   And she
laughed a wild hysterical laugh.

" Well, Nannie," he said soothingly, " now
that you see for yourself how groundless
your fancies are, I hope we shall have an
easy time of it for the future."

But Nannie had made up her mind not to
come round just yet.   So she busied herself
about the child, tossing and singing to it, and
took no notice of his remarks.

Before he could speak again, the telegraph
signal in the adjoining room uttered its
alarum.   On hearing it, Nannie turned very
red, and the more so because she felt that
Criss saw the change in her colour.   With a
faltering voice she said,—

" I thought it was broken."

" It has been repaired in our absence," said Criss. " There are too many poor fellows depending for their bread on my punctuality, for that to be left broken."

And he went to see what messages had arrived while he was out, leaving Nannie with the child to recover at leisure.

Before retiring for the night, Nannie sat beside Criss on a sofa, her equanimity perfectly restored.

" I wish," she said, as she played with his hand, twisting her lovely hair round it, " I wish you did not expect me to be so good. I am sure I should be better, if I wasn't expected to be so. It wouldn't make you bad, being expected to be bad ; why then should I be made good by being expected ?"

" Perhaps it would help you to be good if I were to break out occasionally into a fit like one of yours."

" Oh yes, that it would. Do ! do do it !"

" Well, it did occur to me to-day that it was a good opportunity to follow the example of a person I once heard of, who went to take

charge of a lunatic. The patient was subject to attacks of violence, in which he would
fling about the room and smash whatever
was handy to him. Well, the first time he
did this before his new keeper, who was a
woman of great nerve and resolution, she at
once seized sundry articles of furniture, and
dashed them to the ground, with precisely
the same outcries and gesticulations which he
had used."

Nannie laughed gleefully. "Oh, how I
should like to have seen that!" she cried.
" But what did he do then ?"

" He gazed at her in astonishment, and at
length asked her what she did that for. She
replied that, seeing him do it, she supposed it
was the way of the place, and the right thing
for her to do. The story goes that he there-
upon looked exceedingly foolish, and never
after broke out so again."

" And why didn't you smash the things in
your study this morning, too, if you thought
it might cure me ?"

" I believe my principal reason was that it
was my study. Had it been one of your
rooms now, with all your pretty things about

it, I probably should have done a little smash-
ing."

After a pause she said,—

" I am thinking, Criss dear, that you ought
never to have married at all."

" Well, Nannie, we live and learn."

" I mean that you are too perfect by half in
yourself. No woman can put up with
absolute goodness. There is not sufficient of
the machine about us. Our feelings can't
stand it. They will have relaxation. It is
as bad for us to live with a person who is
perfect, as for a child to live only with grown
up folks. I should be sorry if little Zöe has
no one beside you and me to play with. We
shall be quite old then, and she will want the
companionship of other children. They
learn so much from each other that all the
schools and grown up people in the world
can't teach them. She is almost six months
old now. She will be so dull without any
brother or sister for a companion." And the
sad prospect wrung a little sob from Nannie's
affectionate heart.

Her melancholy forebodings were happily

doomed to disappointment. Zöe was scarcely eighteen months old when the desired play-fellow made its appearance in the form of a little boy.

CHAPTER X.

THANKS to a careful selection of agents and organisation of work, the gigantic operations which Criss was carrying on in the desert, proceeded rapidly and steadily without requiring more than an occasional brief visit from him. In the same way, the work of freeing thought throughout Soudan from the chains of superstition, made progress in spite of the vested interests. When the Emperor had come thoroughly to comprehend the real significance of the claim set up by the priesthood to be superior to the civil government, he had given his countenance to the societies which Criss had created for the spread of popular enlightenment. The battle was virtually won when once the people comprehended that, whatever the object of enquiry, there is but one method—the scientific; inasmuch as it signifies merely accuracy both in observation of facts and deduction of inferences; so that to reject the scientific for any other method, is simply to reject accuracy for inaccuracy.

It was thus that the fictions of so-called history, and the inventions of superstition gradually lost all importance in their eyes, and became but as certain fossil specimens to the geologist, tokens of a lower stage in the earth's development. Students and curiosity-mongers may concern themselves about such things, but they enter not into the lives of those who judge all matters by the criterion of the present.

Talking over these things one day, the Emperor expressed to Criss his surprise that with all his zeal for the enlightenment of the people, he had not attacked the divinity of the Sacred Talisman. " Surely," said the young monarch, " if I am to be a reforming king, and, to use your own phrase, 'of a piece throughout,' I ought openly to discard a superstitious basis for the crown which now affects to justify its existence by Use."

Criss acknowledged that he had thought much on this very point, and believing that the symptoms would disappear as the disease was cured, had judged it best to commence at the other end. "Let us," he said, "be content with gradually developing the intelligence of the people, and they will of themselves then successively shed one superstition after another. Knowledge is the sole proper disturber of faith. No use to extinguish the candle before letting in the sunshine. When once they have knowledge, they will perceive of their own accord that the Sacred Talisman derives all its real value from its intrinsic worth and beauty, and that any mystic addition serves to diminish rather than enhance its lustre."

It was thus that the spirit of Emancipated Europe crossed the Sahara into Soudan, and conquered the chief, if not the last stronghold of superstition remaining in the world. The people and their sovereign understood each other and the unity of their interests, and thenceforth all opposition was vain. The national school, national universities, and na-

tional church of Soudan, became the three
steps in the ladder of the national development ; the appeal in all being to man's present and mature, instead of to his past and
rudimentary. Thus, too, did Europe repay
to Africa the debt owed for Africa's contribu-
tion to the early civilisation of the world ;
and the greater debt owed for the world's
after treatment of Africa. Once a slave-
hunting ground for all men, Africa was now
free in mind as well as in body, and its very
soil was being redeemed as from an hereditary
curse.

If ever the earth had been, as theologians
were wont to declare, morally insolvent, and
capable of rehabilitation only by a vast act
of grace, it was now proving, by its conduct
in Africa, that it had only suspended payment, not become utterly bankrupt ; that,
give it time, and it would pay all.

This last was a train of thought which had
been communicated to Criss's mind during
one of those flights into the Empyrean which
had made the chief delight of his life as a
bachelor. It is only because man is im-

patient with God's slow method of working,
that he denounces Nature as a bankrupt, who
has failed to fulfil his proper engagements to
the great Creditor, and thus fallen short of
the end of his being. ˙ We, who can contemplate such lives as some which have sprung
from the earth—yea, even such a life as this
I am now too imperfectly narrating—may
well hold that, were there no other like it, no
other approaching it for purity, goodness, and
usefulness, one such life is sufficient to redeem
the earth from the charge of being utterly reprobate and fallen, from the condemnation of
having existed in vain, and incurred a sentence
of wrath for having failed to fulfil the end of
its being ; sufficient, therefore, to reconcile its
Maker to it :—just as one magnificent blossom
suffices to redeem the plant that lives a hundred years, and flowers but once, from the
charge of having wasted its existence. Even
if the experience of all past ages of apparent
aimlessness and sterility afford no plea in
justification of existence, the one fact, that
there is room for hope in the future, may well
suffice to avert the sentence men are too apt
to pronounce—that all is vanity and vexation,

and that the tree of Humanity is fit only to be cut down, that it cumber the ground no longer.

With the intellectual emancipation of Soudan, the need of social regeneration became apparent. Here, however, Criss found less readiness to follow an European lead than in other respects. Neither the women were eager to demand, nor the men ready to concede a change in the relations of the sexes, little content though they both were with the existing state of things. A little enquiry showed him that they had never yet learnt to see the essential distinction between social and political equality. The women, too, had been taught, by a comparatively recent event in a neighbouring State, to see the absurdity of their claiming to be legislators at all, when they could be so only upon sufferance, and must at all times be incapable of enforcing their decrees. And the men had taken advantage of the occurrence to laugh to scorn all demands for a change which seemed to involve anything approaching to identity of function in public more than in domestic life.

The occurrence in question was as fol-
lows :—

Several generations ago, a large district on
the west coast of Africa was governed by a
succession of despotic sovereigns, whose sole
idea of religion and political economy was
to appease the gods, and keep down the surplus population, by the periodical celebration
of human sacrifices on an enormous scale.
For a long time the victims of these Kings
of Dahomey (an appellation apparently derived from the Latin *da homines*, "give me
men," supposed to be addressed to the king
by his god) were selected by the merest
caprice. But, as civilisation extended to
those regions, and the sentiments of men
there became softened by the study of philan-
thropy and art, unmeaning caprice gave place
to a system of natural selection, whereby all
the crippled and imperfect specimens of the
population were periodically chosen to be
offered up. The effect of this weeding out
of the inferior types was to produce a race
of men and women as superior to ordinary
folks as the "pedigree" cereals, for which the
hills of our own marine southern suburb were

once so famous, were superior to ordinary produce. The men and women were all beautiful, good, and clever; and never had been known such handsome negroes and negresses.

But as man improved, the gods came worse off; and the priests complained that, owing to there being no imperfect specimens left, the supply of victims for their sacrifices was running short. There was danger, they declared, of some terrible judgment befalling the nation, through the neglect of the public ordinances of religion.

Upon hearing this the King, after holding consultation with the priests, determined upon making a new ecclesiastical canon. By this it was ordered that the selections for sacrifice should be made among the shortest of his subjects, male and female. He trusted thereby both to satisfy the gods, and raise the average stature of his people.

The people, however, after the first sacrifice or two, determined no longer to submit to such a state of things. They were wearied of the exactions of the priests, and they had imbibed certain revolutionary notions unfavourable to monarchy. So one day they rose in a mass, abolished the dynasty, disendowed the church, and established a republic.

So high was the standard of female excellence, that there was no question about women having, under the new regime, an equal share of political power with the men. They had it as a matter of course, and with laudable assiduity did they apply themselves to the practice of parliamentary and forensic eloquence. So earnest were they in the discharge of their public duties, that the men gradually withdrew from public life altogether, as a thing best adapted to women, and occupied themselves with ordinary affairs in the field, the factory, the market, and the home; until every public office was held by women, even the police and the army consisting exclusively of that sex.

Things went along smoothly and well until certain stateswomen of Dahomey, smitten by propagandist zeal, endeavoured to undermine the institutions of their neighbours, on the ground of their unwomanly character. The Emperor of Soudan, whose dominions reached

from the Red Sea to the Sources of the
Niger, had long been anxious to extend his
rule to the Atlantic sea-board. The main
obstacle to his ambition was the prosperous
and easy-going community of Dahomey. The
intrigues of its stateswomen among his own
people supplied him with a pretext for in-
vading it; while the knowledge that it was
defended only by an army of women, made it
seem to him as inviting an attack. He determined therefore to reduce it to submission,
and compel it to acknowledge the authority
which, in virtue of his well-known descent
from Solomon and the Queen of Sheba, he
claimed over all the adjacent regions.

On the approach of the Imperial army, the
women of Dahomey prepared to march out
to battle. The men, concerned at the idea
of danger to their women, offered to go in
their places, saying that whatever legislation
and police might be, fighting a foreign foe who
was really in earnest, was a serious matter.

But the women scornfully rejected their
proffered aid, bade them stay at home and
look after their children and business, and
then marched boldly forth to meet the enemy.

No sooner had they departed than the men met in council. They knew how it would be, and that no time must be lost. It was necessary, however, that their women should receive a lesson. A battle, and therefore a reverse, could not take place for a day or two. So, having armed and formed themselves into divisions, they started after it was dark to occupy the hills which overlooked the plain where the battle was expected to take place, keeping their movements absolutely secret from the army of women.

On the enemy coming in sight, the women with much show of determination, and really making a most gallant appearance, advanced to meet him. The combat was short and sanguinary, that is, to one side, the side of the unhappy Dahomey damsels. Their courage, unsupported by strength, proved to be vain. The Imperial levies, though consisting of a race far inferior in physique, were yet men. They, therefore, could not, under any circumstances, suffer themselves to be defeated by women ; while the women felt, though they did not own it until afterwards, already half beaten through the influence of their own hereditarily-acquired impressions of man's prowess. They were soon in full flight over the plain; and as they fled, the visions of their homes, containing their children and the husbands they had left to tend them, rose before them; and with the army beaten and the enemy advancing, they saw nothing but ruin and slavery for all they loved, or ought to love.

The unhappy fugitives were not suffered long to indulge these bitter reflections. The sounds of battle were renewed. The tramp of a host came near. Whither now shall they flee? Home! How can they face their homes, thus humiliated after all their vauntings?

"What is this? No enemy! but our own— dear—men!! Oh, save us! save, and forgive!"

"All right, all right, lassies"—(they had a few Scotch words in their vernacular. Many of them were literally "Bonny lassies," for they belonged to the province of Bonny, a little to the eastward of their great river, and were not the *Camaroon* mountains, towering thirteen thousand feet high, almost

in sight, a name palpably of Scotch origin ?)
—" all right, lassies," exclaimed thousands of
manly voices, as thousands of muscular arms
were clasped round thousands of delicate
ebony necks. "We knew how it would be,
and took precautions accordingly. You would
go ; but we determined you should not be
beaten too badly. So we placed ourselves
where we could see the battle, and directly
you ran away and the enemy gave chase, we
pounced upon him and cut him to pieces. So
now you can come home, and resume your
functions legislative and protective, without
fear of further molestation."

The women were glad enough to go home,
but from that day forward they steadily
declined to undertake functions which,
through lack of physical strength, they could
only fulfil by sufferance. It was the remem-
brance of this incident that mainly operated
to retard the introduction of the European
system into Central Africa. America, too,
had contributed an example in dissuasion.
For the women of the province of New
England, in an access of religious fervour,
had taken advantage of their being in a

majority at the polls, to create a Popedom of Boston, and elected one of their own sex to the office, and in virtue of the ancient intellectual supremacy of their city, claimed for her spiritual supremacy over the whole continent. It was only by taking possession of the polls by force and reversing the decree, that the men put an end to the absurdity. Thenceforth they have restricted the suffrage to themselves.

Thus, in addition to Criss's other labours on behalf of his African proteges, he undertook to make them comprehend the natural law which seems to assign to men a monopoly of the sphere of politics and legislation, and to restrict women to the social and industrial sphere ; inasmuch as the former is based on force, and the latter on convenience,—a difference of function for which nature, and not man, is responsible.

CHAPTER XI.

SINCE his marriage, Criss had held no intercourse with his spiritual friends. The tenor of his life was inconsistent with reverie. His mind was too much engrossed by his labours or his troubles. On his journeys, which were made with the utmost rapidity, he had things concrete to occupy his thoughts; and ascents for mere abstract contemplation were apt to excite Nannie's jealousy. She was jealous even of the angels, and without waiting for cause given, was ever ready to utter the imperious prohibition, "Thou shalt have no other goddess but me."

Hovering one day in the Ariel over his garden, Criss could see as he gazed downwards, the smooth green sward and embowering trees, and the fair dwelling, and Nannie, the embodiment of all his dreams of loveliness, and Zöe, the fruit of his love for her; the whole forming together a scene of exquisite delight. But the joy with which he contemplated it was instantly dashed by the thought of the serpent which had thrown its coils around it, and converted what should be his home of happiness into his place of torture.

Then recurred to him the vision of his friend the tall angel, and the sweet brideangel, Nannie's prototype; and he wondered whether their experiences had any counterpart in his own; and, if not, in what consisted the secret of their happiness. And as he thus pondered, by a scarcely conscious impulse he drove his car with rapid motion far up into his old ground, the Empyrean. "Tell me, tell me," his heart cried as he ascended, "oh ye blessed ones of the skies, what is the secret of your bliss?"

It was not long before his yearning evoked a reply. For, presently, to his spiritual vision became revealed the well-remembered noble form and serene countenance, and with it the

sweet and sunny face of the fair bride, looking, oh, so like Nannie, but Nannie in her
softest moods, that Criss could not forbear
exclaiming,—

" Soul of my Nannie! canst thou not shed
upon her while on earth some of the sweet
repose and confidence which thou enjoyest in
heaven ? Ye look on me with the same
joyous aspect as of old. Surely ye cannot
be aware of the sadness which darkens my
life ?"

" We know all," replied the tall angel, "and
knowing all, we are glad, even though thou
sorrowest. Thy struggles and thy patience
are not without their reward, even though
they continue to the end. Know that the
task before thee is harder than any that is
given to us. This is thy badge of honour.
It is for thee to prove thyself worthy of it.
Listen to the revelation of the mystery.
Thou and she are products of the same earth,
but of different stages in that earth's development, thou of the later and highest, she of
the earlier and lowest. The inherent force
of attraction which pervades all matter,
organic and inorganic, and constitutes *love*,

has with you proceeded to the advanced
stage, at which love means sympathy and self-
devotion. She to whom you are wedded is
still in that primitive stage in which attraction
is mechanical rather than moral, is of body
rather than of soul—the blind attraction of
otherwise inert masses, like the orbs of heaven
and the constituents of the earth—and is
but the basis of love, rather than the love
which later comes. Only continue to have
patience, and your influence will yet permeate
the system which has hitherto rejected it.
The love that is not self-love ultimately con-
quers all things. It is the sole universal
solvent. It may be in time, or it may be in
eternity."

" The hope may enable me to endure to the
end," replied Criss ; "but it has no potency
to charm her whom I love and would save.
Can ye not give me aught that I may bear
back to her ? Sweet face ! loving heart !"
he exclaimed, addressing himself to the brideangel, who, he now observed, carried in her
arms that which showed him that she too had
become a mother, even a mother of angels ;
" hast thou no wonder-working word of ad-

monition which I may carry back with me ?"

The young matron-angel kissed her child, and then bent her head over against that of her spouse, and after a brief conference with him, said,—

"It is permitted me to impart to thee the secret of all happiness, whether in heaven or elsewhere : the secret that would convert even the dread regions of the lost to a scene of bliss, had those regions not long ago been for ever utterly abolished. Know, then, that the resolve, persistently maintained, to make the best of that which we have and are, would make of hell itself a heaven ; and how much more of earth ! While, ever to make the worst of things would turn heaven itself into a hell. The mind is its own bliss or woe."

"You mean that I have failed to make the best of her ?"

"Nay," responded the other. "The application was meant for her, not for thee."

Criss shook his head as he thought of the uselessness of presenting such a rule to Nannie. In answer to his look appealing for yet further guidance, the tall Angel took him aside, and said,—

" This for thine own ear, for few are equal to the knowledge. Mankind and ourselves are identical in essence. It is the stage and conditions which differ. We have no super-incumbent mass of plasm through which to struggle to our soul's development; and to us such virtue brings but little reward, its practice being so easy. With men it is not so. There are some in whom the divine spark is so dim and chill, that their smallest deed or thought of goodness weighs for much in the everlasting balance. For these things go by proportion. It is not to lack or to badness of heart that the conduct is due through which you suffer, but to narrowness of vision,—a narrowness necessarily inherent in the sex whose special function is maternity. If her mind be too tightly girt with the affections which centre in self and in offspring, to be capable of enlarge-ment in the present, remember that Nature has need of such characteristics to ensure continuance, and that hereafter it may not be so. Yet one word more. With us, like weds only with like, and constituted as we are, we cannot be mistaken in our mutual estimates,

any more than the magnet and the steel. In
your world it is different. There the enve-
lope is ofttimes too dense, and the character
too tardy of development, for the effect of
love upon the disposition to be foreseen. In
such case, to court the irrevocable in marriage
is to rush presumptuously upon fate. But, as
I have already said, the defect with her to
whom you have bound yourself is intellectual,
not moral. Let this, and the certainty that
you are loved utterly, with such love as she
is capable of, comfort and sustain you. Farewell."

On his return from this flight, Criss's
countenance shewed unwonted serenity, and
he said something about the calm airs aloft,
and the force of old associations. Nannie's
suspiciousness at once took fire, for she
had not failed to observe his altered
look. Remembering his old habit of going
up in search of spiritual intercourse, she exclaimed,—

"You have been among those angels
again ! Have you ? I will know ! I won't
have you leaving me for creatures who will

make you think me ugly and bad by com-
parison."

"Why, Nannie, even if I have been among
angels up there, surely you don't want to
make me feel that I am not with an angel
when down here? You can be one when
you like. You can't help having the look of
one. Why not act like one, also?"

"Time enough when I get up there, and
have only angels to deal with. I treat people
as I find them."

"I am rejoiced to find you contemplating
such amendment."

"As what?"

"As will suffer your admission to a region
where jealousy and altercation are unknown."

"Then it must be a very stupid place, and
I don't want to go to it. And I say again,
that if you will persist in cultivating what you
call your ideal, you can't expect ever to be
satisfied with your real, which is me."

Thus, the birth of their second child was
heralded by a renewal of the old wretched
scenes, and it required all the native strength
and hopefulness of Criss's character to keep

him from subsiding into a condition of settled despondency.

" Here is a surprise, Nannie," he said to her one morning after opening a large letter bearing the official seal of the First Minister. " You won't object to being called ' My Lady ' in future ?"

" What do you mean ?" she asked.

" It is through no seeking of mine, you may be sure," he answered. " The Government has appointed me to a seat in the Upper House, accompanying the notice with the most flattering letter." And he handed it to her to read for herself.

It contained a brief but warm encomium on his character and life, public and private, and an expression of hope that he would, by accepting the proffered dignity, let his own country have a yet larger share of the wide enthusiasm for humanity which had inspired his magnificent endeavours for the regeneration of the continent of Africa.

The same post had brought also a letter from Avenil, congratulating Criss on the event to which he, Avenil, had been privy, and saying that although most of the functions of

governing were now-a-days practically vested
in *Bureaux*, yet these wanted careful super-
vision, and that the very consciousness on the
part of officials that intelligent zeal was
appreciated by the Legislative Chambers,
served to secure to the country the benefits of
good administration. Besides, the progress of
civilisation, so far from abolishing the necessity for government, as had once been supposed would be the case, was ever producing
new complications and needs.

" Are there women in it ?" was Nannie's
first query.

" It is a House of Lords, not of Lords
and Ladies, I assure you," returned Criss.

" Well, I don't care, it is all a plot against
me, to take you away." And she lashed herself into a fury.

Criss thought he would try a new tack.

" Well, Nannie, I won't say positively that
it is not so. It is very likely that the First
Minister has heard of me as a poor fellow
trying hard to do his duty in the world, but
so plagued by the childish fancies of a foolish
jealous little wife, as to be utterly miserable

and worn out ; and that it has occurred to him
that he may be giving me some relief by
taking me a little from home, to breathe the
serene air of the Legislature. He is a very
good-natured man, this First Minister of ours,
I assure you. I really should not be surprised
if that was the explanation of it, for you know
that the letter is mere flattery, and that I have
never justified such language by trying to be
a bit of use in the world."

" I hate all talk about use, and duty, and
such stuff. A man who has a wife, has no
business to think of duty elsewhere. What's
duty to love !"

" Well, Nannie, I am truly sorry that you
should be so disappointed in your husband. It
is a great pity we did not clearly understand
at first what your requirements would be."

" You will say next that you are disappointed in your wife, I suppose."

" I should say but the truth. I should
have liked a wife who, on finding her husband so appreciated as to be invested with
the highest honours his country has to bestow,
would be happy with all the joy of which her
loving heart was capable, and by the sweet-

ness of her congratulations, stimulate him to
yet greater endeavours to adorn his life, and
hers, with beautiful deeds."

"Oh yes, you are always hinting that you
wish you had married some other woman.
But you have married me, and I am not one
of that sort."

"I was referring to no woman in particular,
but only to what any woman would do who
had the slightest particle of a heart, and knew
what love meant."

"You used to think me perfect."

"So I do still, as regards the physical and
outward part of your nature."

"Well, and isn't that enough?"

"On the contrary, it only makes your
deficiency in all other respects the more pal-
pable and hard to bear, just as the sight of a
lovely fiend or maniac would be more distressing than that of one whose outward appearance corresponds with its mental condition.
Oh, Nannie! Nannie!" he cried, with a burst
of uncontrolled anguish, such as he had
never before permitted himself to indulge,
"Angel still in form, however fallen in spirit,
is it indeed beyond the power of love, human

or divine, to redeem you from the curse that
enthrals you ?"

" Fallen !" she exclaimed, " I was never
any better than I am."

" True," he replied; " I fashioned my speech
too much according to the ancient traditions.
I ought to have said, ' Nannie, with a capacity
for being the angel you look, will no treatment develop the latent soul within you ?'
Yet in one sense my first phrase was right.
You have fallen from the high pedestal of the
ideal on which my imagination once placed
you."

" Ah, but that was your mistake, for placing
me there."

" It was indeed, and bitterly am I punished
for that one error of judgment."

" What answer are you going to return
about that appointment ?"

" Are you desirous of advising me ?" he
asked.

" I will be good," she answered, " if you
will do one thing to please me. Decline the
Minister's offer."

Criss went into his study, and presently
returned holding out a paper to her.

" I propose to send something of this kind," he said. " What do you think of it ? Isn't that a very good pet name for you in future ?"

She read the rough draft, and said,—

" So I am the ' Domestic Affliction,' and you accept the office with the intention of fulfilling its duties so far as your ' Domestic Affliction' will permit ?"

" Yes, dear—I mean, Domestic Affliction, such is my design."

" I won't be laughed at. I never could bear being laughed at."

" I have tried crying over you, in vain. I must laugh now for a change. It is a change I sorely need, heaven knows ;" and he sighed heavily. " Nannie," he said suddenly, as a new thought struck him, " for the future I waste no more words of reproof or re-monstrance upon you. Whenever you in-dulge in one of the tempers with which you love so to distress me, I shall not utter a word, but only laugh, until you come out of your evil humour."

He had some time since made it a rule never to make mention to her of any person

or object of any kind beside herself. So
habitual had it become with her to vent ill-
natured remarks concerning them, whether
he himself showed interest in them or not.
"Why do you talk to me about them. I
don't care to hear about other folks. You
seem to care about everybody and everything
more than about me." The moment, however, that she observed his reticence, she
charged him with being deceitful, and having
concealments from her. To this his reply
had been,—

"Nannie, it ought to be enough for you to
abuse me. My friends at least should be
sacred; and I shall do what I can to keep
them so, by never referring to one of them in
your presence. You have already by your
virulence cut off almost every possible topic
of conversation between us. So that silence
is really becoming my sole resource."

This time she looked at him half-incredu-
lous and half-frightened, and said,—

"It doesn't distress you more than it does
myself."

"Prove it by your conduct to be so, then,"
he replied, "or I shall think that you take a

pleasure in distressing yourself, as much as in
distressing me."

There was a somewhat longer interval than
usual before she again broke out. Criss
ascribed this, partly to the perplexity induced
by the novel treatment with which he had
threatened her, and partly to the alarm she
could not conceal, at his frequent absences
from home on the plea of attending the sit-
tings in the House of Lords. Nannie had
taken fright lest he should thereby become in
a measure weaned from her. What would
all her explosions effect when met by the
triple shield of absence, silence, and laughter?

One day, to his intense surprise, he came
upon her kneeling beside her bed. No one
could pray for aught that was evil. To wish
for a thing that was good, sufficiently to pray
for it, was, provided it was a thing coming
within range of the spiritual laws, surely to be
far on the way towards its achievement. The
soul must at length be budding !

Filled with joy and hope, Criss endeavoured
to retreat without hearing her words, for she
was praying aloud. But she uttered her
petition with too much vehemence for him to

accomplish this purpose. It was a petition that he and their child, or children, might die before her.

Horror-struck, he rushed towards her, exclaiming,—

" Nannie ! Nannie ! what is the meaning of such a prayer ?"

She hesitated and looked confused ; but at length confessed that she had prayed thus through jealousy lest any other woman should have to do with them in the event of their outliving herself.

CHAPTER XII.

UNABLE to make any way by means of angry reproaches, owing to Criss's persistence in a policy of silence, the unhappy Nannie at length conceived the idea of exhibiting her master passion in deeds. Criss came home one day to find her alone in the house with her child. After a scene in which she had completely lost herself, she had dismissed the entire household at a moment's notice, on the plea that they were in league with their master against her. Her equanimity restored by the performance of this feat, she went to the garden entrance, and quietly awaited Criss's return. In due time he arrived, doubtful of the humour in which he might find her, and was overjoyed at the unwonted sweetness and meekness of her demeanour. Little Zöe was with her, and together they repaired to the house. Criss was surprised at not seeing any servant in waiting, and was about to ring for one, but Nannie stopped him by saying,—

" Is there anything you want, Criss dear ? I will get it for you."

" I only wanted a servant."

" Yes, dear, it is no use your ringing. There is no one there."

" How, no one there ?"

" They provoked me, and I sent them away."

" What, all of them ?"

" Yes, every one. There is not a soul in the house besides ourselves."

" You have sent all my servants away ! And for what reason ?"

" They were my servants, too ; and I am mistress here !"

" Let me hear the cause. I must know how far you were justified."

" Justified ! I hope I may dismiss my ser- vants when I choose, without being 'justified.' "

" No ; no one is superior to justice. I must know all the particulars."

" And if I won't give them ?"

" I shall know that you are in the wrong, and send for them back again."

" You will outrage your wife by doing that ?"

" Pardon me ; I shall be repairing an outrage done by my wife upon justice."

" The idea of putting justice in the scale against your wife ! You make me jealous of justice. You make me hate it and all the other stupid virtues. I shall be jealous of the servants, too, if you take their part against me. Justice, indeed ! No, no. Love, that *is* love, is not for abstractions ; it is only for a person, and does not think of goodness, or anything but that person."

Criss was firm ; and finding that Nannie's conduct had been absolutely causeless, reinstated the whole of his household, apologising to them for the act of his wife. The affection and gratitude they exhibited towards him did not by any means serve to appease her ; but she feared to repeat the act, for Criss declared that he would take her to live at the Triangle, where the servants were beyond the control of individual caprice ; and she hated the Triangle, because he had so many friends in it.

" Nannie," he said to her one day, when this storm had passed away, " I want you to specify to me the causes of your discontent, in order that we may both comprehend clearly what it is that makes us so miserable. Of course, being but mortals, we cannot govern all things ; and you are not so unreasonable as to visit upon me that which is inevitable, and beyond man's power to prevent. Now, I beg you will think over and enumerate to me the various items, great and small, in respect of which you deem your lot inferior to that of the most fortunate women you have known. If you don't like to speak them, write them, and I will see what I can do to amend them. Here's a sheet of paper. Is it big enough to contain the list ? I will number the items," and he numbered the lines with a big 1, 2, 3.

She stopped him when he had got thus far.

" You write it," she said.

" Well, now for number 1 ?"

" My husband makes me jealous."

" Very good ; that is down. Now for number 2 ?"

" You don't deny it ?"

" That part comes afterwards. What am I to write against number 2 ?"

" The same. 'My husband makes me jealous.' And number 3 also. There, now you know all."

" Not quite. We have now got to fill up the explanatory clauses. How does he make you jealous ?"

" Oh, if you don't know by this time, I am not going to take the trouble to repeat it."

" Nannie, I must have some very serious talk with you, to which I insist upon your listening. It is the way of all rational beings to form a certain plan or ideal of the life they wish to follow, and to construct such ideal according to their own constitution of mind and body, and the circumstances by which they are surrounded. Having con-structed such ideal, and entered upon the practice of it, they follow it out to the best of their ability, amending or rejecting, as ex-perience may dictate, whatever interferes with or jars upon it. Now, tell me, have you formed any ideal of life, in the pursuit of which your happiness consists, and from which you endeavour to exclude all foreign and intrusive elements. If you have, I should be most grateful to you for communicating it to me. Nothing would give me greater delight than to help you to maintain the ideal on which your happiness depends, and, if necessary, help you to revise it. Tell me your scheme, and then, if you please, I will tell you mine."

Nannie said that she knew nothing whatever about ideals, and had no scheme, but acted only from impulse.

"I act from impulse, too," replied Criss, " but my impulse prompts me to form and act up to a certain ideal. Having constructed it according to the very best I can imagine, by aid of all the lights I can obtain, that ideal becomes to me as God. This God, I once fondly hoped faithfully to follow throughout the whole of my life, my path at the same time being gladdened by the tender love I should receive from, and bestow on the sweet partner of my home. This God I am resolved to follow to the end, whether I be blest with such joy or not. Should my expected joy be turned into misery, my rose become all thorn, the only question would be, not should I abandon my ideal, but should I give up that which causes my misery? Nannie, in obstructing my ideal of life, you are seeking to withdraw me from God. If I have to give up either, you know me too well to doubt which it will be. Even if I can stand the constant wear and tear of heart, brain, and spirit, which your conduct causes me, my desire for your welfare would compel me to separate you altogether from one in whose love you cannot be happy."

"You would give me up! Then I know there is some other woman——"

Utterly sick at heart, he turned away to leave the room, exclaiming,—

"Better had it been for you, cursed with such a nature, had I left you to take the fatal leap from the burning wreck on which I found you. Nay, better even to have left you to be outraged to death by the ruffians on Atlantika, while yet young and innocent, than preserve you to develop into that which

you have become. Never more let man save
the life of another, unless he is sure that he
is not saving it for a worse fate! I—I have
saved a serpent to poison my own life!"

"Criss! Criss, dear!" called Nannie after
him; "don't go, I want to speak to you."

He returned, looking haggard and ill.

"Be brief and careful," he said; "my patience is nearly exhausted."

"I only wanted to tell you that you go the
wrong way to work with me. You don't
understand women—no men do—or you
wouldn't make such a fuss about us, or let
us put you out so. Because you mean things
when you say them, you think we do so too.
Never was a greater mistake. If you were
to take no notice of my—my—naughtiness, I
shouldn't care to be naughty. But it attracts
your attention to me, and—I like to attract
your attention."

He looked somewhat sternly at her, and
then said,—

"Nannie, I shall take you at your word.
Only, mind this,—if the prescription fails, I
try another."

At the next outbreak, Nannie, who had forgotten the new condition, was astounded to find Criss, instead of lamenting and remonstrating with her, taking it quite coolly, and saying,—

" All right, Nannie darling ; fire away ; I won't mind. I dare say the attack will soon pass off if you give it free vent. But please just stop a moment, and compose those nice lips of yours into one of your charming pouts, while I kiss them. It will be a new sensation to kiss a lovely termagant in the very midst of her fury. No ? Well, if I mustn't reward you with a kiss for the capital receipt you have given me, I will just go out for a bit, and come back when I think the storm is quite over." And he turned to quit the room.

To be taken at her word was the last thing Nannie intended. She was furious at the indifference he had, in obedience to her, so well assumed. Snatching up something heavy that lay at hand—neither she nor Criss ever knew exactly what it was—she rushed towards the door as he was going, and while his back was turned, struck him with all her might on the head, exclaiming,—

" There! that will teach you to outrage a woman's feelings."

So heavy was the blow that Criss was for some moments stunned. Staggering against the wall, he managed to support himself there until power and consciousness returned. She, meanwhile, stood watching him, apparently without having made up her mind as to the next step, for the situation was a new one, and she had no experience to guide her.

On recovering from the first shock, Criss took his wife by the wrist, and led her to a sofa. He did this gently, but firmly, and she made no resistance. Seating himself there beside her, he said,—

" Nannie, a prudent doctor always informs his patient of the effect likely to be produced by any new medicine, so that the patient may not be taken unawares. You omitted to tell me what would be the effect of my following your prescription of indifference to your bad conduct, and thus have, as it were, laid a trap for me. But now that I know so much, I shall be able to take the necessary precautions. There is one point in which I shall imitate the doctor. A long standing complaint is not to be cured by a single dose. I shall continue the treatment you have prescribed, in spite of its having seemingly aggravated the symptoms. So, if you like to let me have the kiss now, which you refused before, please adjust those charming lips——"

But Nannie was obdurate. So Criss added,—

" Pray don't keep me waiting for it, for my head sadly needs doctoring, and your skill in surgery does not include the reparative as well as the destructive branches of the art."

" Nonsense! call yourself a man, and care about a little tap like that! I didn't think you were a coward before."

" Ah, Nannie, even we men have our weak points. Now that you have found mine out, I hope you will be considerate of it. But you wouldn't like to have such a deformity as a two-headed husband, and I certainly shall look as if I had two heads if something is not done soon to allay the swelling. Just feel it." And he guided her hand, unresisting, to the wound.

Nannie had always had a morbid horror of blood. When she withdrew her hand, it was crimson with the blood with which his hair was saturated.

Uttering a scream, she turned away and buried her face in a cushion, and sobbed bitterly.

" I suppose the prescription applies to all outbreaks, whether of reproaches or tears," said Criss, rising; "so while you are indulging yourself, I will go and have my head mended. I should like to have had that kiss first, though."

" You will find me dead when you come back," she sobbed, scarce lifting her face from its hiding place.

" Blissful hope !" cried Criss, gaily. " Don't disappoint it. Au revoir !"

" Poor child," he said to himself after leaving her, " if this does not cure her, the case must be hopeless. And what is to be the end of it ?"

" Doctor !" he said suddenly, while the

wound was being examined in the doctor's surgery, for on second thoughts he had gone thither instead of sending for the doctor to come to him,—" Doctor, what is to be the end of it ?"

" Brain fever and death."

" No, no, I mean for my wife, if she refuses to abandon her wild fancies."

" I was speaking of her. There is no fear for your brain. There is fear, however, of serious inflammation of the injured tissues ; and as you must have absolute quietness, I intend to keep you in close custody here, and let my wife nurse you."

Criss looked wistfully at the doctor, as if suspecting he meant more than he said.

" I see you divine my motive," said the doctor. " It is a twofold one. A good fright, and enforced separation from you, through her own act, will be the best possible thing for your wife. If that lesson fails, you may give her up with a good conscience. Happily the law of the land permits separation without making sin an indispensable formality. And all moral laws combine to dictate such a course to a man in defence of his life, his character, and his proper career in the world. Your usefulness is being sacrificed."

"By the way, doctor, I did not tell you how my head came to be injured."

"And therefore I knew it was by your wife. You would not otherwise have concealed it."

Criss reluctantly consented to go upstairs and lie down, at least for a while; the doctor promising to have Nannie watched, and let Criss know if his presence was called for.

Surprised at his failure to return, Nannie sent a servant to enquire if the doctor knew where he was.

An answer to the effect that he was there, very ill, and must on no account be disturbed, caused Nannie to follow with all speed.

She was ushered into a room, and kept waiting for some time before anyone came.

At length Doctress Markwell entered, and enquired what she pleased to want.

"Want! I hear my husband is here, ill, and I have come to attend on him."

"You are very good, but he is being perfectly cared for, by the doctor and myself."

" But I am his wife, and insist on——"

" Insist on completing your work, and killing him outright ?"

" Out of my way, woman! I shall go to my husband." And she rushed toward the stairs.

" That is quite out of the question. He is far away in a place secure from intrusion, and even from noise. You can neither reach him, nor make yourself heard by him. He has friends who love and respect him, to care for him now, thank God."

" And do you think I do not love him ?"

" It may be with such love as exists among wild beasts, but not with what human beings call love."

Nannie raved awhile, but finding she made no progress, at length went home, somewhat calmed by the suggestion that it would please him best to find that she was attending to her child.

Daily the same scene was renewed, the doctor remaining firm, in the hope of conquering Nannie's wilfulness, and only telling Criss that his wife came daily to enquire if she should come and nurse him. He spoke with no sanguine anticipation of a favour-

able issue for her. "A woman who avows
herself indifferent to consequences," he said,
"and at all hazards persists in indulging her
wildest impulses, is beyond the reach of skill.
It is a growth that is needed, not an alterative. Judging by this characteristic, and
what you tell me of her parentage, I should
say that she has *Calvinism in the blood.* No
man acts fairly by his own life and happiness,
unless he takes into account the character of
the stock with which he allies himself, as well
as the early training of the individual."

The event proved the correctness of the
doctor's prognostications. Nannie soon forgot
the lesson she had received, and showed herself inaccessible to a sense even of the most
serious consequences. Her motto might have
been that of the ancient divinity, "I am, and
what I am I shall be," for she recognised no
law but that of her own unreasoning will; and
self-consciousness and effort at amendment
were altogether beyond her. But the end,
for that came at last, differed somewhat from
that which had been foreshadowed. In the
meantime Criss threw all prescriptions and
endeavours to improve her, to the winds, and

was kind, tender, and loving, as if she had been the best of wives, treating her as a victim of disease, and not of mere wilfulness.

Intensely as Criss felt Nannie's behaviour for himself, it was for her that his feelings were most deeply exercised. Why could she not be as perfect in all respects as she was in respect of the functions specially belonging to her sex ? Surely the old Oriental notion that man only is endowed with a soul, had no foundation in fact. Yet here was one who was a woman of women, and yet to all appearance utterly incapable of moral development. With her, love was all, and of that she could not have enough. So completely was her whole nature devoted to it, that she needed no distractions to enable her to rest and return to its exercise with fresh appetite. It seemed as if sex had so early attained its maturity in her as to arrest and take the place of all other development,—a phenomenon due, perchance, thought Criss, to the tropical climate in which she had been reared.

Pondering thus, long and anxiously, and seeking, as was his wont, to find a place for her in his generalisations of the world, he

became impressed with the idea that hers'
might be one of those natures into which,
through the ministration of pain alone, could
an avenue be opened for the entry of the
lacking soul. " Pain, Sorrow, Repentance,
these constitute, at least for some, the triune
creator of the human soul. The Fall was
indeed a rise, inasmuch as, through the sorrow
that followed, man found, not lost, his soul.
He was made perfect through suffering.
Nannie! Nannie! Am I to be the period
to your initial stage of moral unconscious-
ness, and become to you as a schoolmaster to
develop the inner life within you? The
gospel of grace failing, must I fall back on
the law?"

It was not Criss alone who indulged in the
process of ratiocination. Nannie thought,
too, sometimes, or at least carried on a process analogous to thinking, in whatever it
was that constituted the corresponding part of
her system. Criss's musings, just recorded,
were interrupted by her with the remark,—

" I wish, Criss dear, you would change our
doctor, for one that has not got a doctress
for a wife."

"I am quite in the dark," he said. "Tell me all you are thinking, Nannie."

"I know," she continued, "that you have known him all your life, and look upon him as a great friend, and all that. But now that you are married, things are different. You fancy, I dare say, that a woman doctor is best for a woman, as knowing most about her nature and ways?"

"Certainly. Do you think it is not so?"

"Oh, of course it is so, and that is my objection to them. They know too much, and are apt to be hard upon us in consequence. Every woman is cruel to other women, for women all look upon each other as rivals, and they hurt each other on purpose. I should do just the same if I were a doctress."

"But, without quite agreeing with what you say of your sex," returned Criss, amused in spite of himself at his wife's ascription of her own irrational jealousy to the whole of her sex, "I think an arrangement can be made to suit all parties without my acting so unfriendly and rude a part by a life-long friend. Suppose that for the future Dr. Markwell attends you, and Doctress Markwell attends me?"

" Criss ! you wouldn't, you daren't, have a woman to attend you!" almost shrieked Nannie. " I should kill her, I know I should, and I should be quite justified in it. Besides, that wouldn't answer the purpose at all. For even if she did not see me, he would still be able to consult her about me, and she would be sure to advise what she knew would hurt me. Oh, you don't know what cats we women are !"

" Well, Nannie, you seem determined that I shall not remain in ignorance. Perhaps, after all, the best way will be for us to keep well, so that neither of us require a doctor. I promise you that I will do all I can on my part to avoid calling in Mrs. Markwell."

" You never do what I wish, but always object and argue and make conditions, just as if I was not your wife, and had no right to have my feelings considered. I am sure it is a small enough thing that I want—this time."

" A small thing ! that I should show gross rudeness and ingratitude to people to whom I owe so much——"

" Owe ! why you have paid them well——"

Here Nannie paused, for she saw upon her husband's face an expression of intense

disgust at this last utterance. For his anger
she cared little,—that was not incompatible
with love. But she did not want to incur his
contempt. His reply convinced her that she
had gone too far.

" I will see what I can do to meet your
wishes," he said coldly, and rising to leave the
room. " Perchance it may be better for you to
be placed in a position wherein you will be
free to choose your own line of action in all
things, without reference to me. For it is
clear that we cannot agree upon a common
point of view."

If Criss seriously contemplated a separation from his wife, it was not for his own
sake. The very femininity of her nature bound
him to her so completely, that he would
endure anything that was painful to himself
merely. But he could not imagine her as
equally wrapped up in him, while she persistently abstained from making the slightest
effort to mould herself to his wishes. He
began to think that she would be both
happier and better without him, perhaps in
some other and more congenial association.

The thought was agony to him. But for her good he would dare anything.

A conversation which took place that same evening at Bertie's served to mature his thoughts on the subject. Avenil and Dr. Markwell were there together with Bertie and Criss. As all were old and attached friends, all rejoiced in the news which Avenil had brought from town. It was to the effect that his youngest sister, Bessie, had, after little more than a year of separation from her husband, begged to rejoin him, and her prayer had been accepted.

It had come about in this way. For the first month of her self-imposed widowhood, Bessie had seemed to rejoice in her freedom. She owned herself, however, surprised at the lack of warmth with which she was received in society. She could not understand why she should be looked on coldly when she had only exercised an undoubted right. Being strong and brave of spirit she determined to treat this as a matter of little moment. At the same time she could not help admitting to herself that she was more lonely than she

had expected to be ; and she was very glad
when, at the expiration of the first six months,
her child came to spend the second half of
the year with its mother.   It was a little girl,
and Bessie took to it with an ardour that
astonished herself.   Her period flew as time
had never before flown with Bessie.   She was
in despair when the time came for the child
to return to its father.   Seeing her tears and
agitation, the child remarked,—

" Papa cried too when I came away from
him."

This put an idea into Bessie's head, but
before acting on it, she determined to see first
how she was affected by the renewed separation from her child.   A short time was sufficient to show her both that she herself could
not be happy without it, and that she had
inflicted on her husband, who evidently loved
the child as much as she did, a far greater
degree of pain than she had been aware of.
Her motives for desiring a separation in the
first instance now appeared to her to be of
the most trivial and selfish character; so
much so, indeed, that she doubted if ever she
could be forgiven and received back.

Forgiven and received back! Should she stoop to this, and put it in the power of people to say that she repented only because she had failed to get another husband?

The struggle was bitter, but it was brief. She was an Avenil, and therefore had a strong heart as well as a strong head. "What is it to me what people say, if I think it right, and choose to do it?"

In this mood she wrote to her husband :—

"I have been selfish, but I knew not how selfish until now. Am I beyond your forgiveness?"

His reply found her nearly distracted by the suspense. When she read it, all was joy. It ran thus :—

"I love you still as ever. If you can be content with such love as mine, come."

To this the little one added, in her large childish hand, "Come, dear mamma," with a rude circle drawn beneath, in which was written the words *Two Kisses*, to signify that

she and her father had each imprinted a kiss
on that spot.

"There is no doubt what would have been
the result under the ancient law," remarked
the doctor, when Avenil had finished his narrative. "The unhappy couple, unable to separate legally, would have dwelt together in
discontent and misery until death did them
part, or degradation worse than death."

"The child was the real reconciler," observed Bertie.

"And a very proper function too, for a
child," said the doctor, "and one fully recognised by the law when it left Nature free to
operate unembarrassed by artificial enact-
ments."

"Would it not have done as well," suggested Criss, "for them to have tried a
temporary separation before completely dis-
solving their union ?"

"Most assuredly not," said Avenil. "It is
true that but for the child, either or both
would probably have contracted a fresh marriage within a year. But only the conviction
of the reality of the separation would have

worked such a change in the mother. She
had long thought that all was over. Her very
despair served to redeem her. A separation
which she could regard as terminable at any
time would have produced no such salutary
effect."

"Redeemed by despair," repeated Criss to
himself, as he walked, pondering, homewards.
"And I had been thinking of sorrow and
suffering, but without the other dread element, as a means of saving my own poor
child, and evoking an inner life. Would a
like regime answer with her? Certainly not,
unless she voluntarily undertook it herself.
And this she has no motive or desire to do.
For she is not really discontented. Her idea
of love is that of a rapid alternation of con-
flicts and reconciliations. It includes a spice of
hate as an essential ingredient. The Avenils
have heads as well as hearts. They can
commit mistakes and repent, and be the better
for them. My poor Nannie has no head to
go wrong with, therefore none to repent and
amend with. Were she to find herself sepa-.
rated from me for any fault of hers, so far
from seeing and owning her fault and im-

proving, she would, like a wild animal, tear herself in pieces with rage. Strange arrest of development! in all that relates to the fundamental fact of her being, she is, and knows herself to be, perfect. But of any superstructure that ought to be raised on that foundation, she comprehends and tolerates nothing. What a power she would have been in an Eastern Hareem How perverse the fate that made her mistress of an English monogamist's home! And yet—and yet—I doubt whether she is unhappy. Well, if it be so, and the suffering is all mine, let it be so. I can endure. And I shall endure it the better if I believe that she does not suffer likewise."

So Criss reasoned himself out of the idea which had suggested itself to him, the idea of separating from Nannie. He did not know that after his departure from the cottage, his friends discussed his case, and came to a not very different conclusion. Avenil had asked the doctor whether he thought Bessie's history would suggest to Criss a practical remedy for his troubles. The answer was,—

" He will think of it, and reject it as not suited to the patient's constitution."

" I meant for his own comfort," added Avenil.

" He will consider nothing but her good. His Christianity consists in being faithful to his convictions even up to crucifying-point. He knows that such a measure as a separation would induce in her acute cerebral inflammation, to which madness would probably supervene. No, what she requires is a religion. I doubt whether anything else will reach her complaint."

" Well, doctor," said Avenil, " if you have in your pharmacopœia a religion capable of curing a woman of jealousy, the sooner you prescribe it the better. But I confess that I never heard of one."

" I can guess," remarked Bertie, " what our dear boy himself would say on that point. He would say, ' If love fails, can religion succeed ?' "

Relief came in a way unanticipated and undesired. It was the time of midwinter. Their second child was a few months old.

Nannie had retired to rest alone, for Criss had gone to see Bertie, who was again attacked with sudden and severe illness. Despite her promise to go to bed as usual, she had sat up till past midnight waiting for Criss's return, as he had promised not to delay after the dangerous symptoms had abated. At length she yielded to the entreaties of the nurse, and went to bed.

Criss remained with Bertie until the remedies had worked the desired change. It wanted yet several hours of daylight when the doctor pronounced the danger over for the present. Criss then started off in a bitter storm of wind and sleet to walk home.

He had not gone far when he thought he heard a faint cry, as if calling some one. Seeing nothing, he continued his course, but at a slackened pace. Presently there was a sound of steps, accompanied by a cry of agonised despair. This brought him to a stand, and while standing something rushed upon him, carrying a burden, and just as it reached him, fell to the ground, uttering a name which he did not catch.

" My poor creature, who and what is it

wandering at such a time and in such
weather ?" he exclaimed, in a pitying tone,
and stooping to raise the prostrate figure.
" A woman ! half clad ! and a child too !
Come, let me raise you up, and put this warm
cloak round you, and if you have no other
and nearer refuge, let me support you to my
house, where you shall be cared for. It is
enough to kill the little one, to say nothing of
its mother, as I suppose you to be."

" I was forced to bring the child, or it
would have cried, and awakened the nurse ;
and they would have prevented me from
coming——"

" What, Nannie !" cried Criss, thunder-
struck on recognising his own wife and little
son.

" Yes," she continued, " it is Nannie. I
was so wretched and miserable without you,
and so frightened to think that—that—but
see ! see ! the child is warm, oh, so nice and
warm. I kept him so closely wrapped up in
my shawl. He is quite warm, though I have
been waiting for you to come so long, so long.
I thought my feet would have been frozen.
Yes, take and carry him for me. Now I have

found you I can forgive you all—all. And let me hold your arm, and we will soon be home. Oh, not so fast, I cannot keep up."

Whatever Criss might feel, it was no time to expend words either in anger or pity. With much difficulty he got them home, and having directed the nurse, whom he found just awakened and half distraught with fright on discovering their absence, to put both mother and child instantly into a warm bath, he went to his study to summon Dr. Markwell.

A long time of sadness followed. First, the little one went ; and then Nannie's fever from cold and—I was about to say—remorse, but to this, indomitable to the last, she would never own. The fever from cold and excitement settled on her lungs, and brought on a consumption which defied all skill.

During its progress, Nannie acknowledged to Criss that in her heart she had always, even while behaving her worst, believed firmly in the depth and genuineness of his affection. Yet, so ingrained in her nature was the sentiment of jealousy which had led to such lamentable results, that even to the last she busied

herself in contriving for Criss plans of dissuasion from a second marriage.   In this view
she said to him one day,—

"Criss, dear, I will tell you a reason why
you ought never to marry again.   Your love
is of the kind that would drive any woman
mad.   By-the-by, doctor," she said suddenly
to him, "am I mad ?   Must I not have been
mad to have had such impressions as I had,
if they were not true ?"

"No, my dear lady.   Everyone is liable to
impressions, fancies, or ideas ; for such things
constitute an element of thought.   Madness
consists in acting upon mere impressions,
especially when they are devoid of probability, and incapable of verification."

"Tell me," she said to Criss another time,
"what was your feeling when I was behaving
so ill—when I struck you, for instance ?
Weren't you in a great rage, and longing to
knock me down ?   I know I wished you had—
sometimes.   I wanted to feel that I had good
cause to be naughty."

"My first feeling was for you, my poor
darling.   I thought of the agony of unhappiness you were laying up for yourself."

" Yes, yes ; that's quite true. It was so ;
only I was too proud to let you know it.
But what was the second ?"

" The second was a reflection which gave
me vast comfort. I felt that your confidence
in my love must indeed be unbounded, when
you could subject it to such severe tests."

" I should like to live, Criss. But no ; it
is better I should die. You will always love
me if I go now. If I were to live, I should
do something much worse than I have done
yet,—something that would make you hate
me. Oh, I know I should ! The demon is
too strong in me for me ever to be good.
Unless—unless—I could remain always as I
am now. Do ask the doctor, Criss, if he can
keep me alive just as I am, without getting
any better or any worse. I think the consumption agrees with me. I am sure I feel
better and happier, and more good-like than
I ever did before I had it. I wonder if I
could behave worse were I to get well. I
hope, Criss, it was not I that caused our little
boy's death. Oh, if I did that, I am a mur-
deress already !"

" My dearest Nannie, put such wild and

dreadful fancies out of your head," he exclaimed; for he was resolved to keep from
her the agonising truth that the child had
indeed been killed by the exposure on that
terrible night. Had her own life not been
threatened, such knowledge might have been
necessary as a lesson against yielding to her
uncontrolled impulses.

Avenil rejoiced in Criss's bereavement
almost as much as he had rejoiced in his marriage. It is true, he regarded Nannie as the
most perfect specimen of simple womanhood he
had known, for the potency in her of the instinct
of monopoly, and the absolute concentration
of all the faculties of her being upon the
main function of her sex. It was by this light
that he was wont to interpret the ancient
legend of Eve, which represents the woman
as taking the initiative. In Avenil's view,
derived from a profound study of natural
history, Nannie would have been less perfect
as a woman had she possessed a greater
width of intellectual comprehension.

He thought, moreover, that he discerned
a certain affinity of character between the

husband and wife, in that each possessed a
highly emotional temperament. Criss's reli-
giousness, he held, would have endangered
his sanity, had it not been counteracted by a
sound education and training. It was through
the lack of such discipline, that Nannie's emotions had driven her to the borderland of
madness. Now that men have ceased to
coerce their wives by superior physical force,
or to allow priests to do it for them by means
of spiritual terror, or society by might of conventional law, the only safeguard that women
have against the tyranny of their own emotions is to be found in the training of their
imitative faculties, or whatever it is in them
that corresponds to the intellect in men.
That the entire female population of the
globe had escaped coming to utter grief, he
held to be due to the strong hands of the
male part. The necessity of being cruel
only to be kind, thus, to Avenil, accounted
fully and satisfactorily for the ancient regime
of " injustice to women." Avenil, it should
be mentioned, is not a married man. He has
never, he says, found time.

Finding Criss continuing too long incon-
solable, his faithful friend, the doctor, ventured one day to remark, by way of remonstrance,—

" You are thinking of her as living in all
her surpassing loveliness and irresistible
vivacity, and . without the drawback of the
excitability which marred her perfections.
Endeavour rather to think of the fate that
awaited her and you, if she had lived. You,
perhaps, murdered; she, certainly in a mad-
house. If ever foolish woman was bent
upon driving herself mad, she was. If no
other, let the reflection that you are both
spared this, be your consolation."

Nannie's last words had been,—
" You wanted Nature, and you got it—
pure, genuine, unadulterated Nature. Did
you not, Criss dear ? Own you did, and say
that you liked it so—better than if it had
been civilised and tame. I know how it is,
Criss. You thought you were wedding sunshine, and you wedded a volcano. Never
mind, Criss ; it will soon be an extinct one.
Perhaps it will some day come to be, for you,

like that one we could see from our place in
Soudan, its rugged sides covered and hidden
with beautiful plants and flowers. I hope,
Criss, you will let your ugly memories of me
be covered up by fair ones. I can't bear
there should be anything ugly about me, even
when I am dead. Don't cry for me too long ;
I should never have been any better were I
to live a thousand years. I am worse than
the volcano. I am more like the lightning,
that can only blast and destroy, and never
produce anything good or beautiful ; though
you did tell me once that the lightning and
volcano have the same origin as the sunshine.
Perhaps they have ; I don't understand anything. I only know one thing, and that is,—
I should never have been any better, never,
—unless you beat me. Oh, Criss, Criss !
why wouldn't you beat me ?"

BOOK II.

CHAPTER I.

COME now to a stage in my story
which I would gladly omit, or at
least touch upon very lightly. It
relates to myself and my connection
with the Carol family. That connection, it
is true, is sufficiently close and important to
make some reference to myself indispensable.
I am, nevertheless, strongly of opinion that a
far less detailed account would better tend to
maintain the harmonious proportions of the
narrative, while it would certainly be infinitely
more agreeable to my own feelings, to say
nothing of those of my readers. Having,
however, a coadjutor in the task, and that
one whom my readers will assuredly recognise as entitled to dictate, being no other than
the daughter of Christmas Carol, backed by

powerful friends,—I find myself overruled, and compelled to submit. When I state that I persevered in my opposition until sundry chapters of my own biography had been actually composed for me—the said chapters being altogether monstrous and impossible, being the work of one far too favourably disposed towards me to be critical —I trust my readers will consider themselves fortunate in having only this modicum of egotism thrust upon them.

In following my avocations as a student in the library of the British Museum, it happens occasionally that I come across old books of imaginative fiction, in which the writers have set down their views of the condition of society when civilisation should have advanced far beyond the stage reached in their own day. English, French, German, and American writers all tried their hand at such forecasting of the future ; but, ingenious as were their attempts, there is one respect in which their sagacity was wofully at fault :—most of all so in those of France, where ecclesiasticism and political organisation bore greatest

sway; and least of all so in those of America,
where individual freedom most prevailed.

The error of these prophets consisted in
their regarding physical science as destined
to dominate man to such an extent as to
destroy the individuality of his character, and
mechanise his very affections. It is true that
the writings to which I am referring belong
principally to a period when the human mind
was yet so much under the influence of rigid
inflexible systems of thought in religion,
politics, and society, as to make it very diffi-
cult for men to realise the true nature and
functions of the new power which was to
regenerate the earth. They thought that in
exchanging Dogma for Science they would
merely be exchanging one hard master for
another. As it had ever been the aim of
Dogma to crystallise, if not to suppress, all
the humanity of human nature ; so it would,
they supposed, be the business of science to
deprive character of individuality, and life of
contrast and variety, by making all men alike,
and converting the world into one vast
Chinese empire. My story will have failed
in respect of at least one of its main ends, if

it does not enable my younger readers to see that under the reign of Science, Civilisation has come to consist, not in the suppression, but in the development of individual character and genius, to the utmost extent compatible with the security and convenience of the whole mass.

It is by many a bitter experience that the world has learnt that systems of organisation are no substitute for personal development. The Ruler, whether he wields the sceptre, the lash, or that yet more dire instrument—spiritual terror—is until the principle of Fear be discarded altogether for that of Knowledge, but a driver of slaves who will some day break out into disastrous revolt. If I have dwelt much on the Emancipation and its great achievement—the liberation of the National Church from its dogmatic basis, and the consequent preservation of its organisation, prestige, and resources to the State—it is because this was the event which alone rendered truly rational education possible in England ; the event which, by combating and ultimately defeating the spirit of *Jesuitism* in all its various manifestations—ecclesiasticism,

communism, socialism, and trades-unionism—
and so destroying from among us the love of
drilling and dictating to our fellows, and of
making ourselves a rule to others, constituted
the basis of all our subsequent advances. So
long as the State supported this spirit in the
Church, it was powerless against its action in
society. Our unreserved acceptance of the
axiom that the prime function of government
is the maintenance of liberty, religious, political, social, and industrial, was indispensable
to the fulfilment of the modern era. The too
long deferred assumption by Government of
the functions of the *Policeman*, strong, ener-
getic, and ubiquitous, was the death-blow to
the tyranny alike of priest and parent, peasant
and artisan.

Then for the first time in the world's history was a people really free, free to think,
to speak, to work, to win, and to enjoy ; free
from every tyranny—saving one.

Saving one : for there was, and is, an exception to the rule of entire freedom ; an
exception founded in the very constitution of
our own nature, even the tyranny of the
Affections, — a tyranny requiring, not less

than any other, the restraint of a developed
intellect. What mattered it to me that I
dwelt in a land of liberty, where the whole
order of society was contrived expressly to
secure my freedom, when feelings which were
a part of myself, and from which I could not
escape, demanded the sacrifices which cost
me so dear ? What mattered it that the law
of the land would have justified my evasion
from all family ties, on the plea that I had a
right to my own soul, and that my soul, thus
bound, was not my own, when the law of
affection within me compelled me to remain,
even at the price of my utter self-annihilation ?
Useless indeed, in such case to argue that the
individual *ought* to assert himself, and be true
to the lights vouchsafed to him. The only
comfort possible for those who have not the
resolution to declare themselves in youth, and
sever the connection ere it has become con-
firmed by time, consists in looking forward to
a day when the progress of enlightenment
shall have involved even parents such as
those now in the Remnant, and when the
inalienable right of children to their own souls
shall be fully recognised by the most indomit-

able sectarian. It is to my former associates
of the Remnant that I say this, on the chance
of my pages finding admission within those
adamantine walls. Those who are of the
Emancipation need it not. They have
already long since recognised it as a sacred
duty to encourage their children to form and
follow their own judgment in all matters of
opinion, and in all their professions to put
Conviction before Compliance. It is thus in
reality as well as in theory, that the Emancipation repudiates the world-old practice of
human sacrifice.

How my own eyes were first opened, and
how I first met Christmas Carol at the Alberthalla—two events which are always associated together in my mind—have already
been related. My story brings me now to
the time when the acquaintance thus begun
was to bear its due fruit.

It may seem strange that I had failed to
recognise one in whom my family had so
special an interest. The fact is that, although
in my childhood I had heard my father speak
of an adventure which had happened to him
in his youth in connection with an iceberg

and an infant, the story had, through my
mother's reticence, faded into a dim tradition.

It was about eight years after that first
meeting before I again saw him. In the
interval I had become a man, and his name
had grown familiar to me as that of one of
our most honoured citizens, and not less
remarkable for his origin and wealth, than for
his character, genius, and achievements.
Since our first meeting I had always kept him
vividly before me, watching, though from a
distance, every movement in which he bore a
part. I longed intensely to know more of
him, but was withheld by my constitutional
shyness and a not unjustifiable pride, from
making any approach. There would be
nought, I felt, between two men placed in
positions so different, save favour from one
and obligation from the other.

Besides, the exclusiveness of my family
ties operated as an impassable barrier to
detain me from the great outer world. I had,
at the time of which I am now speaking, a
twofold object in life, namely, to keep from
my mother the knowledge both of the change

which had come over my religious opinions,
and of a serious reverse of fortune which had
befallen me. Each of us had derived from
my father an income sufficient for all our
moderate wants. But I, being ambitious of
something beyond this, had put my money
into speculative investments, and lost it. My
mother's income was untouched, but it sufficed
only for herself. I hardly knew which intelligence would most grieve her, the loss of my
money or the loss of my religion; for I was
far from being convinced that her piety was
of that unpractical sort which leads some persons to regard spiritual prosperity as a satisfactory counterpoise to temporal adversity.
However, either would cause her acute
agony, and embitter the remainder of her
days. I determined, therefore, to make no
apparent diminution in the cost of my living,
but to earn the means by steadfast labour.
Even here my adherence to the Remnant
stood in my way. I could not look beyond
our own circle either for the objects or for the
rewards of my work. All must be done
within the narrow limits of the Sect, or my
labours would be regarded as unhallowed,

and myself as reprobate. Even in making excuses for my newly found faculty of industry, I was forced sometimes to sail so near the wind as to feel very uncomfortable at the deceit I was practising. It was only by persuading myself that the bigotry in deference to which I was acting, was a sort of madness, and that it is lawful to deceive a madman for his own benefit, that I managed to reconcile myself to the necessity. If I committed a wrong in thus acting, the compensation must be found in the motive that prompted it. It was solely to spare my mother the misery which a knowledge of the truth would have caused her.

That she ought not to have experienced unhappiness at my following my own judgment, and asserting my own individuality of character, I am well aware. But it is a fixed idea among parents in the Remnant, that they are so infallibly right in their own notions respecting all things, that their children are hopelessly lost if they venture to differ from them. So saturated are they with a sense of the Absolute, as to have no comprehension whatever of the Relative. It may be asked why, when I had learnt to rejoice in my new-found liberty of soul, I did not seek to make my mother a sharer in my joy. The answer is easy. I did not think she would be damned for not believing as I did. Whereas she was certain I should be damned for not believing as she did. I could not be guilty of the cruelty of letting my mother know—at least in this life, where I could prevent it—that I was to be damned.

I preferred that she should think me stingy. I know that she thought I had become most unreasonably economical, and absurdly in-dustrious. I know, too, that she feared the effect of my devotion to my work on my soul's prospects. Absorbed in worldly labour, I was apt to be withdrawn from God. This was a favourite notion in the Remnant. All doing was so likely to be wrong-doing, that they held it better to do nothing than run the risk of doing wrong. My art underwent a change. The demand for paintings of sacred subjects being confined to our own sect, the sale was too small to answer my purpose. Besides, I had become tired of producing them. With my emancipation from bondage

I had learnt to recognise the beauty and
sanctity of humanity and its affections. I
painted a series of tableaux illustrative of my
new phase, but unfortunately was not sufficiently careful to conceal them from my
mother's watchful eyes. She reproached me
for venturing so near to the " broad path." I
took them to the publishing office of an Art
and Literature Association of high standing,
and whose agent I had heard well spoken of.
Telling this man my business, I enjoined him
to keep my name absolutely secret.

He was greatly surprised at the request,
and said it was quite a new thing to him that
an artist should refuse the fame of his work.
" Was it diffidence?" he would venture to ask,
"because there was sufficient talent in the drawings to render such a sentiment misplaced."

I told him that my reasons were connected
with private family circumstances, which,
while they induced me to work for pay, compelled me also to work unknown—unknown,
that was, to my relatives.

" Your work would be much more valuable," he said, " with a name to it."

I replied that I was aware of that, but for

the present, at least, must be content to be a loser to that extent. Of the two, *fames*, not fame, must be my lot for the present.

He explained to me that he was only a publishing agent for an Association of Authors, and that it would be necessary to submit them to a committee. " We never," he continued, " issue any work unless it appears to us to possess a certain amount of merit, and likely to be acceptable to some class of society,—what class does not matter to us. Our *imprimatur* being sufficient to insure us against loss, we are able to publish everything at our own risk, taking only a small percentage of the profits to reimburse outlay and expenses. And as artists do not care to quaff their wine out of the skulls of their brethren, the rest goes to the author."

I left my work with him, and a few days afterwards received a note saying that the committee had been struck not only by the originality and execution of the designs, but also by the continuity of idea existing between them, and were willing to publish them in a volume, if I would provide a story to which they might serve as illustrations. But a

name must be attached, though not necessarily the real name.

To this I consented, and adopting a
pseudonym, set to work in the new direction.
I was by no means satisfied with the result, but
the committee and their agent were. The
time thus occupied, too, was so long, for I
got on but slowly, that only the hope of succeeding in laying a foundation for future
success reconciled me to the privations I was
forced to undergo rather than get into debt
for my living. My mother noticed my loss
of appetite at home. I led her to believe I
had eaten something while out. I really had
lost my appetite, for I was sick and harassed
with delay and apprehension.

The publication paid for itself, but brought
me little beyond some favourable notices in the
press. The agent, however, assured me that
I had made a good beginning, and my future
work would be sought for ; and encouraged
me to persevere in both lines. In the meantime I was at my wits' end to keep up appear-
ances at home. My clothes became too shabby
for me to appear at the social gatherings of
our set ; and I had to make every decent

excuse I could think of for not accompanying
my mother to the place of worship where
alone, in her view, a soul could gain a certainty of safety.

My physical strength became so reduced,
that my mind was affected also. I actually
envied those who had none to grieve over
them if they committed suicide. The object
of all my endeavours being to save my
mother from sorrow on whatever score, suicide
was one of the last things I could, consistently,
contemplate.

One day I called at the publishing office,
and told the agent that if he could not dispose
of the originals of my drawings I would take
them home. He said that some enquiries
had lately been made by a person who would
only purchase them on condition of knowing
the artist's real name. He added, with a
somewhat singular expression of countenance,
that if he were in my place he should think
twice before refusing the terms. But that of
course pride must be paid for.

" Pride !" I exclaimed. " Do you think it
is pride that keeps me back ? Listen, and
I will tell you all."

He listened, and I told him all, even to
how my mother lived in comfort, while I lived
with her and starved, rather than let her
know either that I had forsaken her creed or
lost my own fortune.   He seemed really interested, and said he had often heard of such a
sect as the Remnant, but had no idea such
narrowness could have survived to our day.
After a good deal more talk, he repeated his
advice to let him impart my name to the lady
who had taken a liking for my drawings.

" A lady!"

" Yes, one of the *P.M.s*.   And I assure
you, you could not find a better set of
patrons."

" *P.M.s!*   And what may they be ?" I
asked.

" Ah, sir, I forgot.   You have lived out of
the world, and are not familiar with things
that everybody else knows.   The *P.M.s*
is a colloquial term for the well-known
heiresses' club, and means *Particular
Maidens*.   The members are all young ladies
of fortune and station, who decline the association of merely fashionable and wealthy
men, and make a point of looking out for

young men, especially struggling ones, of
genius and aspiration, either to adorn their
club gatherings, or to bestow themselves
upon in marriage. I assure you, sir, you may
do worse than dispose of your works in that
quarter—or yourself either," he added after
a pause, smiling.

I was still so incompletely emancipated
from the traditions of my sect, that I regarded
all such associations of women with a considerable amount of repugnance. I knew
what they would be if composed of such
women as there were in the Remnant. While
the idea of a marriage for money, or of being
indebted to a woman for the means of living,
excited my scorn and horror. I said as much
to my friend, for such, since I had told him
my story, I felt him to be.

He replied that there was many a nice
woman who would be only grateful to a man
whom she could love and esteem, for taking
care of herself and fortune, and not consider
that he was under any obligation to her.

I confessed that I myself had never been
able to see why it should not be so, but that
I had never yet discovered a woman whom I

could credit with the possession of sufficient
magnanimity to make such a position toler-
able to a man's self-respect. "I consider," I
added, "that the highest compliment that
can pass between the sexes, is for a poor man
to marry a rich woman. A man never credits
a woman with such largeness of heart as
when he puts it in her power to suspect him
of having mercenary motives in his love."

I observed that as we conversed, he paused
from time to time to write something, but
without breaking the thread of our talk.

"Many a man thinks in the same way,
while he is young," he said. "But I never
knew one regret the money, however much
he regretted his choice of a subject."

"Well," I said, "as I should marry only
for the love that would make a home of my
home, such an association as you describe
would be to me a constant sore."

"The money would enable you to buy
poultices."

"I am afraid my poultice would prove a
blister," I answered, laughing, and departed,
leaving my paintings for further considera-
tion.

CHAPTER II.

HE notion of combining whatever talents I possessed into an harmonious whole, became especially pleasing to me. I had always been a dabbler in verses, and now glanced through my portfolio to see if I had any which would bear illustrating. The artist who is not a mere imitator, I held, ought to be both poet and painter. There can be no reason why both modes of expression should not be united in the same work, as music with singing. I found some which suited me, and having illustrated them to my fancy, took them to the office. To my intense astonishment, the agent at once wrote me a cheque in payment, far exceeding anything I had dared to hope for, even after long waiting.

" Soul is up in the market just now," he
said, smiling. "Always put soul into your
work, and it shall be equally well paid."

" May I ask any questions ?" I enquired.

" Nay, I cannot encourage such inconsis-
tency in one who insists on being himself
anonymous."

He then made me an offer for the originals
of the illustrations already published. I
gladly accepted it, and left his office with my
head in the clouds.

The removal of one difficulty served to
launch me into another. I could obtain payment provided I could work. But my
mother's failing health made her terribly
exacting in her demands upon my time. She
could not bear that I should be away from
her side ; and to be with her meant to be
idle, so far as any paying work was concerned.

At length, becoming worse, she was re-
commended to pass the summer at a favourite
watering-place in Iceland. It was only by
means of the money I had earned that I was
enabled to accompany her. So we went, she
little dreaming on how slender a chance my

acquiescence had depended, and I shuddering at the narrowness of my escape from being compelled to reveal to her my poverty in justification of my refusal.

I had long wished to see Iceland,—that country without a fellow, in the fantastic peculiarity of its formation. I was curious to witness the giant contest between vol-cano and glacier; to live beneath a sun that, for the whole summer long, scarcely sets, and to know also what it is to breathe perpetual darkness. Modern physiologists had excited in me a desire to test, in my own person, the truth of their theories respecting the influence upon the human system of the prolonged presence or absence of sunshine. I was now to see it tested upon her in whom all my affections were centred,—even upon my mother, whom, for the heart-complaint that was wearing her down, the doctors were sending to pass the summer in Iceland ; for the new cure for such malady was Sunshine. Patients not too far gone to be able to endure the journey, were believed to have been kept alive for years by shifting their position, every six months, from one Pole to the other, where

Sanatoria had been made for their reception, the journey between being performed by air.

The physicians hesitated to subject my mother to the longer journey,—to the North Pole. Neither could she with safety travel by aerial conveyance. So we went by sea, in the Scot-and-Ice-land Ferry, and took up our abode on the northern shore of the island. I told the agent of my intended journey, and its cause, and of the satisfaction it gave me to be able to devote the first proceeds of my new work to such an object. I said also that I feared my work would be sadly hindered by the interruption.

He expressed a contrary opinion on this head. I was just the man that ought to travel. No new scenes or experiences would be thrown away upon my work. Let me only give myself wholly up to nature, but "nature with a soul," he said, and I need have no anxiety on the score of success in art, whether written or painted. "In the meantime," he added, "if you can manage to send me any light or fugitive pieces struck off in the intervals of heavier and more permanent work, I will at once remit the pro-

ceeds to you. You must not be above
the production of what the trade calls *Pot-
boilers ;* such things have a use above
that which their name indicates. They
are a relief and rest from more serious
work, and enable the artist to return to it
with increased zest. It is not given to mortals to live always up to the same high pitch.
The tension must be loosened sometimes.
The universe is not peopled exclusively with
archangels. The artist, as well as the ordinary man, must relax his morals. In other
words, he must condescend to consider what
other people think and like, as well as what
he himself thinks and likes. Granted that
he stoops in so doing ; well, self-abasement,
in moderation, may be a judicious alterative.
It has often happened that in stooping, he
has stooped to conquer. Let me give you an
instance. Once upon a time, somewhere, I
believe, about the beginning of the Emancipation period, there was an author who had
expended himself in elaborating his highest
ideals of faith, and art, and life, for the elevation of his countrymen. His work was admired by all, read by many, enthusiastically

praised by some, but bought by so few (for
they were books of instruction, rather than
amusement), that the author himself was in a
fair way to starve ; for, like you, he had
hazarded and lost the fortune he had in possession when he started on his literary career.

"Well, he determined to make the public
not only admire and praise him, but *buy* him.
So he set to work and wrote a tale, which,
while outwardly affecting to illustrate all the
excellences of his country and times, was in
reality a bitter satire upon the follies and
shams of society. The rich bought it because they found in it an apotheosis of *Dives;*
the poor, because it exalted Lazarus. The
sceptical bought it because it exposed the
fallacies of the priests ; the pious, because it
upheld the Church and respected religion.
The Materialists bought it because it represented matter as the basis of mind ; the
Spiritualists, because it described mind as
pervading and shaping matter. The old
bought it because it gave them ground of
hope for an hereafter ; the young, because it
bade them make the best use of this world,
without reference to a life beyond. The

men bought it because it bantered the foibles of women; and the women, because it upheld their claims as against the men. The ignorant bought it because they could understand every word in it ; and the learned, because it contained an esoteric meaning discernible only by themselves.

" So the money poured in, and the author became rich ; but the richer he became, the more ashamed he was of himself and of his kind. He had at last won success, but at the expense of his ideal. Was Satan, then, he asked himself, really the god of this world, and the human conscience but a delusion and a snare ?

" Now, mark the moral. By thus making himself, as it were, 'a little lower than the angels'— by condescending, I mean, to an ideal more closely approximating to that of the general—he had caught *the public*, and established a *rapport* which resulted in creating a demand for his earlier writings scarcely inferior to that for his later one. As the teacher of a new faith may work vulgar miracles to draw the attention of the crowd to his pure doctrines, so his higher work had

been advertised by his lower. I make you a
present of the hint ; and wish you farewell."

"One word," I said. "What was the title
of his successful book ? I have much faith
in titles."

"As it consisted," he replied, "of ideas
already floating, more or less vaguely, in
men's minds, and flattered the most popular
feelings, it was very appropriately called, *In
the Air ; or, Made to Sell.*"

The early part of my sojourn in Iceland
was passed in making acquaintance with the
natural wonders of the island. Now that I
had the most invigorating of all diets—Hope
—to animate me, I could yield, without reserve, to the elation produced by the bracing
airs and strange scenery. My mind, thus
renovated, rose to new inspirations, in which
the ordinary and the commonplace seemed to
me to have no part. I had one great work
on hand, partly literary, partly artistic ; but I
did not fail to follow the advice I had received, and send home from time to time the
stray sparks which were struck out in its
elaboration. Yet in these I did not con-

sciously derogate from the high ideal to which
I had devoted myself. And I was most
thankful to be spared the necessity for doing so. My publisher was true to his word,
and thus I was enabled to live in comfort,
and even to provide my mother with little
luxuries which had otherwise been unattain-
able. It seemed to me as if some good
genius must have been watching for my arrival at the lowest depth of despair, in order
to seize the moment and make it the turning-
point of my destiny.

On one point I was somewhat uneasy. I
had, in one of my moments of depression,
made a rough draft of an advertisement, containing an appeal for aid on behalf of a
student of art, who, having lost his own fortune, desired the means of continuing his
career, if any could be found to support him
until success should enable him to repay
them. It was not so much that I seriously
thought of sending such an advertisement to
the papers ; I had drawn it up merely to see
how it would look when written.

This I had lost, and for some time I was
under an apprehension that my mother had

found it. Even when I at length ascertained that this was not the case, I continued to be uncomfortable at the idea of its having got into strange hands. I shrank from the thought of such a revelation of myself.

At first my mother seemed to derive benefit from the change. But towards the end of the summer she was so decidedly worse that I felt convinced the end could not be far off. I now found myself in a very curious frame of mind. Tenderly attached as I was to her, and ready to devote myself utterly to the promotion of her recovery, I was constantly pondering whether her recovery would be the best thing that could happen either for herself or for me. The more I hated such a line of thought and drove it from me, the more it persisted in haunting me. It was only by resolutely refusing to regard them as my own thoughts, and treating them as thoughts naturally occurring to a disinterested by-stander who might be weighing all the pros and cons of the situation—much, in short, as Providence itself might be supposed to do— that I kept myself from being made exclusively miserable by them.

One fact I could not hide from myself. For our lives to be perfectly happy it was necessary that my mother and myself be in perfect accord, without any concealments. I knew the fatal influence of the system of intellectual suppression pursued in the Remnant, too well not to be aware that a change on her part was absolutely impossible. All intellectual independence was regarded as the result of worse than moral depravity. And the knowledge that I had come to certain conclusions which did not coincide with her own traditional ones, would be accompanied by the conviction either that I had been changed at nurse, or that she had given birth to a child of wrath, with whom she could have neither part nor lot in the future world.

But, however potent my motive for concealment, and however merciful to her my resolution, I could not be blind to the fact that such habit of deception was far from agreeable to myself, or favourable to my moral health ; and also that it was very doubtful how long I should be able to maintain it. Determined as were the efforts of the Remnant to shut out every gleam of light coming from the outer

world, they could not always succeed in pre-
venting names and deeds and words of note
from penetrating into their retreat. The
literary agent knew my name, if nobody else
did, and so long as it remained a small name,
would probably keep it secret. But what if
it grew to fame ? Was my whole career to
be sacrificed, and I sink to lower aims and
lower work, for the express purpose of eluding
fame lest my name might reach my mother's
ears ?

It was thus a singular conflict of opposing
feelings to which I was at this time a prey.
The very consolation I derived from success
was embittered by the thought of the pleasure
my mother was losing through her inability
to sympathise in that success. I learnt then
that the concealment of our joys from those
to whom we are profoundly attached, is far
more grievous to endure than the concealment of our sorrows. If grief is halved by
sympathy, assuredly joy is more than doubled.

That in the event of my mother's death,
her income would become mine, was a motive
which, I rejoice to say, scarce thrust itself at
all before me. It was only my resolute

resolve to drive all such canvassings away as the snares of an enemy, and combine to the very best of my ability, my work with her health and comfort, that carried me through this distressing period, and when at length she departed, prevented my having any feeling regarding myself, save the satisfaction of having sacrificed myself to the utmost for her.

Her death was doubtless accelerated by the unusually severe climate of that season. As I have since learnt, it not unfrequently happens that large masses of ice become detached from the coast of Greenland and drift across to Iceland, where they form into a compact body, and for the time utterly ruin the climate of the island. This was the case the year that we were there. What we ought to have done was to go on to the clear warm seas at the Pole ; but my mother could not or would not make another move. Even the homeward passage by sea was closed by the ice, and it was useless to propose to her to travel by air.

After her death my grief and sense of isolation were very keen. She had many friends and I had many acquaintances, in the Remnant. But from all these I was now cut off. I was not one of themselves, and did not intend to claim a place among them under false pretences. That was over for me. But elsewhere I knew not where to seek for a friend, scarcely for an acquaintance. The ordinary engrossments of men of my age, love and marriage, were beyond the reach even of my dreams. Putting all my work aside, I allowed the Arctic winter that was closing in upon the isle to enshroud my spirits with a more than Arctic dreariness. A volume of narratives of the Arctic explorations of old times—when men were forced to content themselves with traversing the surface of the earth without cutting the knot of their difficulties by soaring into the air—helped to beguile but not to cheer those dark days. Having some of my father's papers with me, I chose that season for looking through them. Among them I found some lines indicating that he, too, had vividly realised a like situation, aided no doubt by his recollections of his own early adventure. The lines in question had been suggested by the story of an explorer who had lost the whole of his com-

rades, and remained prisoned fast for succes-
sive years from all possibility of returning to
his home and his love. It is, however, less
for any intrinsic quality than for their connection with our story, that I have thought
fit to insert them here, and consented to do
the same with those of my own which follow:—

" As Arctic voyagers muse upon the zone
    Wherein they gathered up their sunny youth,
    And glow again amid the chilling scene—
    A brief relapse of joy, when pent among
    Those everlasting solitudes, to think
    The sun still shines afar, but not for them,
    And ne'er for them may shine : to know that soon
  . Those joyless seas may be a burial place
    From which their frozen souls will hardly mount ;
    Or should they chance to 'escape their shattered bark,
    'Tis but to drag a drear existence on,
    A Lapland life instead of genial home—
    Thus must I lead a dull inferior lot,
    No warmth without, but that one fire within,
    Cherished as life from the surrounding cold."

When I resumed work I illustrated these
lines—supplying the sun's absence by an
electric-lamp—and forwarded the result to
the literary agent by aeromotive, a regular
service being maintained throughout the year.
I could not make up my mind to return home
myself, simply because I felt that I had no

home to return to, and was not yet equal to
the task of seeking for one. I was not unhappy; for the release from the constant
anxiety and concealment of my later years,
operated to balance my sense of bereavement.
Moreover, my mother had been spared the
pain of knowing that I was an apostate. If,
where she was now, the knowledge had
reached her, she would with that knowledge,
know also the sanctity of the instinct and the
resolve which had guided me. For do not
the dead see things "with larger other eyes
than ours ?"

The keenness of my sensations under my
new position, and the weird wildness of the
country, brought me several inspirations
which I duly turned to account, never failing
to receive immediate and satisfactory returns.
I thus came to welcome any occurrence which
afforded me a vivid idea, that might be both
poetically and pictorially expressed. It was
an additional satisfaction to me to find that
some of my lines were deemed worthy also of
musical expression ; and that, through the
same kind agency, I gained an advantage from
their publication as songs.

I mention these details by way of leading up to an incident which not only provided me in the first instance with a subject for illustration, but ultimately affected the whole tenor of my life.

The summer sojourners in Iceland had all taken flight. I thought myself the sole stranger in the island. My principal delight after the day's work was over, was to go down to the shore and watch the masses of ice growing into bergs, as by the pressure of the ice fields which now extended far beyond the horizon, it was forced up into conjunction with the glaciers which descended from the mountains. The aspect of the fantastic shapes, and the strange groaning and travailing of the massive crystal, as if in the throes of a new birth—the whole at times transparent with magical light of blue or green, or glistening and crackling as it reflected the gleams of the Aurora—exercised a fascination which I found it hard to shake off. The natives, either from use or from dulness, were insensible to the scene; and my enjoyment therefore was wont to be a solitary one.

One evening, however, I detected a figure moving on the ice at a perilous distance from the shore. After watching its movements for some time, my eyes became sufficiently accustomed to the dim light to perceive that it was a woman. Now and then sounds reached me as of one declaiming, and the idea was borne out by the motion of the arms. She passed near me on her return to the shore, but without perceiving me, and to my surprise I recognised her as one of the visitors of the past summer ; an exceedingly lovely girl of some eighteen years of age, whose variableness of expression had often struck me, when I had passed her walking with her companion, a fair handsome middle-aged lady.

The aspect of this girl produced on me the impression that she was suffering from some heart-affection, but not of the kind for which a sojourn in Iceland is commonly pre-scribed. When her thoughts were diverted from herself, it seemed to me, no maiden could be more bright and gleeful. Absorbed in contemplation, she was the picture of woe.

After seeing that she had returned safe to

her dwelling, I suffered my imagination to dwell on her, and her strange manner and reckless action ; and to frame an hypothesis which found vent in the following verses :—

A maiden stood on a sunny shore,
  Where the waters rippled brightly,
And tender breezes gently bore
  The song she sang so lightly.
" Dance as thou wilt, oh happy sea !
My heart leaps up in gladder glee,
Far brighter rays within me shine,
Than gild that dazzling breast of thine !"

A woman stood on a rocky shore,
  Where the waves were driving madly,
And scarce was heard amid their roar,
  The strain she poured so sadly.
" Rave as thou wilt, oh, driven sea,
Thou canst not match my agony :
On sharper rocks than thou dost know,
My all of joy is dashed to woe."

Again, beside an ice-bound shore,
  Where the ocean, frozen, slumbers ;
The wintry breezes slowly bore
  Her low and measured numbers.
" Freeze to thy depths, oh marble sea ;
This heart will colder, harder be !
Nor sun, nor wind, again can move
My stricken soul to life or love.",

Having illustrated these verses, making for
the last one a fac-simile of the scene I had
witnessed, and which had suggested them, I
sent my work home; but could not so easily
dismiss this lovely, and evidently unhappy,
girl from my mind. I sought for opportu-
nities of seeing her close. I ascertained the
name she and her companion were known
by, but it was strange to me. So far as was
apparent, they were mother and daughter, in
retirement for the daughter's health.

My glimpses of them were but rare, and
the scene on the shore was not repeated.
However, I saw the young lady close
enough and often enough to become deeply
impressed with a sense of her beauty and
worth. Whether or not I was absolutely in
love, I do not undertake to determine. I
tried to think that I was not, but that only
my fancy was touched, for the idea of coining
my heart into money was infinitely repugnant
to me. I have reason to believe, however,
that the most popular table-book in London,
and particularly in the Triangle, before that
winter was over, was one which contained the
two sets of verses just given, with illustrations

in which the colour-printers had admirably
seconded the artist's designs ; and also a third
set, upon the significance of which the reader
may form his own hypothesis ; the whole
volume being entitled *Winter Reminiscences
of an Artist in Iceland.*

Why haunt me when I know thou dost not love me?
  Why haunt me when thou never canst be mine?
'Tis not thy bliss to fill the air above me
  With gleams of visions false e'en while divine.

Why wilt thou still diffuse thy look and tone
  O'er every spot my wand'ring footsteps seek ?
Why leave me not to tread my path alone,
  Unwatched by eyes of thine, so pure and meek ?

Yet, no, I cannot with thine image part,
  Or cease with thoughts of thee my soul to fill.
Thou dost not love me, perfect as thou art ;
  But I love ever, therefore haunt me still !

CHAPTER III

N my return to England, I took up a temporary abode in the *Intellectual quarter* in London, and removed thither all my effects, thus completely forsaking both the neighbourhood and the associations of the Remnant. I was enabled to do this without regret, regarding, as I did, that sect as the cause of all the miseries of my life, foremost among which stood the barrier erected by their superstition between my mother's soul and my own. Regarding, I say, this sect as worshippers of a demon, and believers in human sacrifices, sacrifices of minds and consciences, if not of bodies, I was not disposed to endure the remonstrances which my apostasy was sure to evoke from my mother's friends. As I had no notion of letting my purpose be affected by anything

they might say, I thought it best to escape the annoyance of listening to them, by holding myself altogether aloof.

But, while thus abhorring the system to which I had been subjected, and resenting the unhappiness it had caused me, I found myself hesitating to declare positively that the evil had, in my case, been an unmixed one. I fancied that I could trace the development of anything that might be valuable in my disposition or character to the hard training I had undergone in the conflict between duty and affection. But though, for me, from evil had been educed good, it did not follow that I should be kindly affected towards the evil. Besides, might not the character which was capable of such alchemy, have been, under other and more favourable conditions, far more advantageously developed ?

I said something of this kind one evening, when in conversation with a little group of men whom I met in the salon of the Triangle. My friend, the literary agent, was a member, and on my returning to England free from all motive for concealment, he introduced me to the Club as a visitor. The evening in question was the first I had ever passed in society that was congenial to me. I was so little accustomed to the ways of the living world, that, while observing with all my eyes, and listening with all my ears, I scarcely ventured to exercise my tongue. In fact, I felt very much as I imagine one to feel who, after being blind for years, first opens his eyes upon the things around him.

But the kindness I met with when it was known that I was not merely the artist of several of the favourite books then lying on the salon table, but one of the family of Wilmers who had been so long and favourably known in the Triangle as the close friends of the Avenils, and their early associates in the guardianship of the young Carol whose name had since been in the mouths, and whose character in the hearts, of all men,—the kindness I hereupon met with broke down all my diffidence and reserve, and made me feel that at last I had come among my own kind. A stray soul welcomed to bliss by sympathising angels, could not feel otherwise than I did on that ever-to-be-remembered evening.

The group to which I had been introduced
·consisted of my host, Lord Avenil, and some
of his sisters, the son of Mistress Susanna, a
fine young fellow of nearly my own age, who
bore his mother's name, and another, who at
first sat writing at a table near us, and to
whom my host said he would presently introduce me.

Young Avenil apologised for the absence
of several of his aunts and cousins, who he
said would otherwise have made a point of
being present to welcome me, but were under
an obligation to attend in some distant town
.at the opening of a new Triangle, of which
they were the architects and decorators.

The questions with which I was plied
respecting the history of my family since their
secession from the world to the Remnant, and
the nature of the life led by the sect, gave me
plenty to say without betraying my ignorance
of things in general. It seemed to me that
the man who sat at the writing-table, though
apparently intent on his occupation, was not un-
observant of our conversation. His face was
in shade, and I could not discern his features,
but I thought that I could now and then

feel a gleam, as from lustrous eyes, resting
upon me.

I had, in reply to their friendly curiosity,
been describing the feelings with which I
now regarded the sect from whose blighting
influences I had effected my escape, very
much in the terms I have set down a little
above. The stranger had caught my words,
and apparently found some chord in his
nature struck by them. For the first time he
joined in the conversation, saying, without a
word of ceremony,—

"Your own nature has divined the spell
with which once upon a time I found myself
obliged to conjure away the demon of nega-
tion for a young friend in circumstances not
altogether different from your own. He, too,
was an artist, but through ease of circumstance was idle and luxurious. He believed
in the superintendence of unseen influences,
and reproached them for not interfering to
save his life from being wasted, but had not
strength of resolution to make the necessary
effort himself. Prayer, as you doubtless have
often observed, is very apt to take the form
of requiring another to do our duty for us.

In the wantonness of idleness he took to
gambling, and did not leave it until he had
lost the whole of his fortune. He was now
more than ever bitter against those whom he
considered as the guardians of his fate. But
he had not leisure to indulge his bitterness.
Necessity compelled him to turn his hand to
toil. I watched, but said nothing. His work
succeeded, for it was very good, and he made
a name and a fortune. 'I have beaten the
spirits,' he said to me exultingly. 'When I
trusted myself to fortune, they let it turn
against me, and ruin me. I have re-made
myself by myself! No thanks to my kind
guardians !'

"' And you are happier now,' I said, ' than
before your adversity ?'

"' Happier and better. It has made me a
man !'

"' And without your providential spirits
having any hand in it ?'

"' Why, they turned the luck against me,'
he said.

"' But if you are so much the better,' I
asked, 'can you say the luck was really
against you ?'

"' Ah, I see!' he said, and added, ' It is a case, I suppose, of things working together for good. But I did not know that I could be called one who "loved God."' "

" And of course you suggested that perhaps the love was the other way," interposed Lord Avenil, addressing the speaker. " But, my dear Carol, do you know that that is the most immoral story I ever heard even you tell. It is a direct incentive to gambling. What will our new-found friend here think of the company he has got among. Come, I am glad you have done writing. I have been wanting to introduce you to the son of your earliest nurse, Lawrence Wilmer, in whose arms you were first dandled on the iceberg, and to whose ingenuity you owe your very name."

" I am glad you did not introduce us before," said the other, rising and advancing to me with the look in his eyes and over his whole countenance that I well remembered,— the look that perforce drew all men to him. " I am glad you did not introduce us before. The delay has enabled me to *wish* to know the son of my dear lost Lawrence Wilmer

for his own sake, as well as for his father's.
But you must know," he added, " that unless
I am very much mistaken, this is not our first
interview. Am I not right ?" he said, addressing me.

" It is so, indeed," I said, " and that first
interview has never left my memory. But I
did not think our few moments' converse in
the Alberthalla could have enabled you to
remember me. Besides, I was but a lad
then."

" Ah," he replied, " I read souls, not faces
merely. And I am disposed to think that
though your face be older, your soul is
younger than it then was."

The conversation which followed was of
a kind the most grateful to me, making me feel
that from an adventurer and an outcast, I had
become a member of a family and a home.
I was about to retire with the friend who had
brought me, but was stopped by Carol, who
said that he would take it as a great favour if
I would accompany him to his own rooms, as
he wished some further converse with me.
He then walked some steps with the literary

agent, and I heard him on parting from him say,—

"My dear sir, you have performed my commission to my complete satisfaction, and earned my warm gratitude. He seems all that you have described him."

Then rejoining the party, he said,—

"Avenil, you will forgive my appropriation of our friend for the rest of the evening. There is much that I wish to talk about with him. Indeed, you must not be surprised if I grudge you a large share of him at all."

Thus I found myself installed more as a son than as a stranger in the private dwelling-rooms of Christmas Carol. The only change I noted in him was that he seemed at times less buoyant of manner and spirit than he had at first appeared to me, as if through the burden of some present grief. But this was only when silent. In conversing he was all himself.

To my surprise, what he took most interest in was my recent sojourn in Iceland. The few questions he asked about my previous life indicated a familiarity with it altogether unaccountable to me at that time. The incidents of my stay in Iceland, which had suggested the verses and illustrations already referred to, were the points on which he seemed specially anxious to gather information.

I told him all I had seen that bore on the subject, not concealing the sentiment which had been evoked in my breast. I acknowledged my ignorance as to how far love or compassion predominated in me. That the damsel was as pure and good as she was beautiful and sad, I declared that I had no manner of doubt, and should esteem myself fortunate could I have the privilege of consoling her.

He said that, artist-like, I had evidently constructed a complete romance upon a slender foundation; and that it would probably be better for my career as an artist, as well as for my happiness, were I to keep to my dream, and shun the reality. He added with a smile, which appeared to me to have in it more of sadness than of mirth, that he hoped I was not seriously smitten.

I replied that I did not think I was at

present, but felt that I might very easily become so, inasmuch as I was singularly amenable
to the influence of faces and voices, and had
considerable faith in my faculty of divining
character by them. I added that the conclusion which now seemed to me most probable, was that this young lady was suffering
as much through her own act as through that
of another, for I had read in her looks con-
trition as well as resignation ; yet nevertheless,
I was convinced that even if she had herself
committed a wrong, it was not through lack,
but through excess of heart ; and I could forgive any act that had been thus prompted,
no matter what it might be. " In the sect in
which I was brought up," I added, "we pro-
fess to hold in high estimation a book which
we are taught to believe is now-a-days little
considered by any but ourselves,—not that we
understand it, or get much beside harm from
it. I have, however, always found a mighty
significance in one of its utterances. It is
this :—' Her sins, which are many, are forgiven her, for she loved much.' My own
people, following, I believe, some of the early
Christian fathers, hold that this sentence

ought to be expunged, as having an immoral tendency. For me, it contains the whole gospel. I cannot bring myself even to regard as sin that which is done for love, and not for self."

I suffered myself to be led on in this way, seeing that, so far from attempting to direct the conversation into another channel, he was at least content with the topic. To myself it was so great a relief, after my life of suppression and reticence, to utter my mind freely to one whom I intuitively recognised as capable of comprehending me, that I experienced not the slightest pang at such departure from my habitual reserve.

" We have left far behind us," he remarked, in an absent meditative manner, "the times in which love and sin were commonly linked together in people's minds. Sin now-a-days is associated with breach of contract, or unfaithfulness, both being forms of selfishness. However imprudent an individual may be in yielding to the impulses of love, there is no sin unless some one be defrauded thereby, though, of course, there may be much inconvenience. This is now the popular and

general sentiment on the subject, and humanity has gained infinitely in happiness since
its adoption. Still, I can imagine a nature
so constituted as to feel bitter mortification
on the score of having ignored the judgment
of those who were entitled to be taken into
confidence,—a mortification that would constitute repentance, and make a second and
like defect of conduct impossible."

I said that it seemed to me that the sentiment of mortification was scarcely possible
except in one who had previously regarded
himself as infallible. That as I read life, it
is a series of lessons from experience; by its
very constitution involving error, even error
moral as well as intellectual.

" The old contest," he said, manifestly
speaking to himself rather than to me, " between experience and intuition. I have taught
her to follow heart alone, even as I myself
have followed it, and nought but sorrow has
come of it, sorrow to both of us."

Here the clock seemed to have caught his
eye, for he said, looking at it,—

" There will be no more signals to-night.
I thank you for having given me your com-

pany thus late. To-morrow, if I am not
making too great a demand upon you, I shall
have matters of greater interest to impart to
you. I quite long for the time when you will
become a resident with us. Avenil says it
will be like old times to have a Wilmer once
more in the Triangle. I wonder whether you
will find in any of his nieces a charm to counteract your recent impression."

I left him after promising to return for
breakfast, and having a sort of instinctive
conviction that he knew more of me than he
had said, or than I could comprehend, and
that there was a relation between our lives
scarcely to be accounted for by the fact of
his having been first nursed by my father on
the iceberg. His conversation also perplexed
me. Though coherent in itself, it seemed to
vary its object, and point sometimes to himself, sometimes to my own recent experience,
and sometimes to some third person with
whom his mind evidently was much occupied.

CHAPTER IV.

REAKFAST was already prepared when I arrived at the Triangle next morning. But my host was engaged in an adjoining room, and I had leisure to look round the apartment into which I had been shown. It was the same that I had been in over night, a small and sumptuous chamber, evidently a favourite one, to judge from its comfortable home-like aspect, and the character of its conveniences and decorations.

Being an author and an artist, my first glances of course fell upon the books on the tables, and the paintings on the walls. I was pleased rather than surprised to find among the former my own little works. My feeling was one of blank astonishment, when, on going round the room, I found, carefully set up upon a stand by themselves, the whole of the originals of my published drawings, excepting the very latest ones.

While I was gazing in wonder at them, Christmas Carol entered, and apologised for his delay, saying that he was always at the mercy of his telegraphs, and required his friends to make allowance for him. Perceiving what I was looking at, he smiled, and said that his daughter had been so much pleased with the first specimens she had seen of that style, that she insisted on purchasing the whole of the series. " I suspect also," he added, " that she was a little piqued by the artist's refusal to allow his name to be made known."

" Does she know it now ?" I asked.

He said, " No ;" and in answer to my question whether she was a member of the club known as the P.M.s, he said " Yes," but that she rarely availed herself of her membership, being of a somewhat too retiring and domestic disposition to feel quite at ease in the Common room of a club. " Poor Zöe," he added, " she

has been very much out of health of late, and
has caused me great anxiety. I should like
to introduce my dear nurse's son to her. Can
you spare yourself to me to-morrow for the
day to run down to my place in Surrey ? She
is staying there at present, with her step-
mother. We shall find there one whose
affection for your father will make him overjoyed to see you,—Bertie Greathead."

We agreed to start about noon ; and in the
interval I was made acquainted with so much
of his history and pursuits as enabled me to
comprehend his exact position, and feel that
he was in no way a stranger to me. I was
introduced also to the room in which he had
been occupied when I arrived. It was a very
large one, and entirely taken up with the
machinery whereby he controlled the various
works he had in hand. In addition to numerous telegraphs, there were surveys and
drawings of various portions of the Sahara
and the Mediterranean coast ; with tables
showing the exact progress of the work, and
the areas already covered with water. So
vivid were his descriptions of the various
processes and details that I could almost

fancy myself in the country itself, and a witness of his mighty efforts to raise half a
continent to a higher stage of development,
physical and moral.

About the man himself there was a simplicity and genuineness of character which
showed him to be greater than all his works.
I said something in reference to the tenets of
my old sect,—to the effect that his life was a
refutation of their doctrine that the world
was so much more fit to be damned than to
be saved that only supernatural interposition
could accomplish any improvement.

He replied that a work called divine, as
Creation, if anything, is undoubtedly entitled
to be, would fall very far short of deserving
such an epithet unless it contained within
itself the elements of its own improvement :
but that, for his part, he had a strong objection to the use of such words as *divine* and
supernatural, as being apt to mislead. People
might as well talk of the super-divine origin
of Deity, as of the supernatural origin of
Nature.

His reference to his second wife excited in
me unbounded astonishment. Not that I had

the slightest right to indulge such a feeling,
but the whole aspect and character of the man
were so strongly suggestive of steadfast un-
dying constancy to a cherished ideal, that I
could not reconcile myself to the notion of his
being married again. And I soon found
myself fancying that he was of my mind in
the matter, and had not succeeded in recon-
ciling himself to it, now that it had been done.

I was somewhat disappointed to find that
our excursion into Surrey was to be made by
railway. I hoped to have gone in the famous
Ariel. To my enquiry whether he was as
fond of aerialising as formerly, he said that
his enjoyment depended on his being free
from anxiety. He could not bear to burden
the light airs aloft with mortal cares and sorrows. "The soaring bird," he said, "is
always joyous, whether he utter himself in
song, or be mute in ecstasy. When he has
griefs which will not be left behind, he re-
frains from making the ascent."

His longest journeys, however, compelled
him to travel as of old, in his Ariel. He
was expecting to make one shortly to Africa.
The works, which had been so many years in

operation, were now approaching completion. He would take me with him to see the first re-union of the Mediterranean and the Sahara, after their long divorce. Already so vast a quantity of fresh water had made its way through the excavations as to form several considerable lakes, and many regrets had been expressed at the.prospect of their freshness being destroyed by the introduction of the sea. The people who uttered these regrets, however, had no conception of the real magnitude of the contemplated results. Already, he said, had the elongated *Shary*, in its issue from Lake Tchad, formed a broad and deep channel almost into the heart of the Sahara, and deposited myriads of acres of rich alluvial soil at a level somewhat above that which would be reached by the new sea. The people of Timbuctoo, delighted with the result of the experiment, had themselves proposed to turn the surplus waters of the Niger into the desert. Even from the far off low-lying coast lands of Senegambia and Guinea, came the cry,—

"Take our surplus waters, and relieve us of the perpetual curse of inundation and fever."

The Emperor's engineers had reported that their portion of the work was fast approaching completion, and that the waters of the Mediterranean and Red Seas would soon mingle in the bed of the Desert. In the meantime, he added, the work of raising the people of Soudan above the reach of ignorance and superstition, has been wondrously facilitated by their contemplation of, and participation in, the vast physical operations in progress. Superstition being the product of man's ignorance of nature and of its capacity for being subdued and controlled, the sentiment soon vanishes in presence of a Science that teaches him that he is himself the appointed conqueror of nature. The people of Central Africa are now well advanced on the path which our own civilisation struck out for itself.

My meeting with Bertie Greathead, whom we took in our way, was of the most delightful description. The kind-hearted old man seized upon every point about me that served to remind him of my father, and made me feel at once that my life was enriched by the acquisition of another genuine friend. He

·detained Carol for some minutes after I had parted from him, and then called me back to say I might always count on a home and a welcome whenever I chose to come that way, which he hoped might be often.

On reaching our destination, Carol's demeanour indicated more uneasiness than he had hitherto betrayed. As it certainly was not owing to any ill news he had received of his daughter from Bertie, I was at a loss to account for his manifest preoccupation ;—unless, indeed, it arose from the recollection of his first marriage mingling with reflections upon the second.

It must be remembered that at this time his domestic history was altogether unknown to me. That his second choice was a good one, whatever the first might have been, fairly augured from the handsome presence and gracious manner of the lady who met us at the door, and after affectionately embracing him, welcomed me, with an admirably proportioned admixture of precision and effusion. If in this first meeting there was anything that jarred on me, it assuredly was not on the side of the lady ; but rather on that of her husband, whose manner struck me as colder and more restrained than was appropriate either to the occasion or to the persons concerned.

" Our darling Zöe," said the lady, amiably overlooking all defects, " would have rejoiced to unite her greetings with mine, but her sad health causes her to keep much aloof from society,—even from mine, though living in the same house. I do trust, my dear Christmas, that your visit will quicken her spirits somewhat."

" Where is she? Is she well enough to see us?" he asked, in a tone that betrayed no intention of being beguiled into using more words than were absolutely necessary.

" She is in her own apartments, and, of course, able to see her father," replied the lady, marking the last word with a strong emphasis.

" Then I will ask you, Amelia, to entertain Mr. Wilmer, while I go and see her. He is an author and an artist, and so will be able to appreciate your descriptive and creative talents."

Before he could leave the room, the door opened, and a young lady entered, and, run ning up to Carol, embraced him tenderly. She was tall and fair, but with dark, expressive eyes, and a somewhat Oriental cast of countenance, and about nineteen years of age. Great as was her beauty, it struck me that the illness from which she was suffering must have enhanced it by the delicacy it imparted to her aspect.

Leading her towards me, her father said,—

" Zöe, I have at last captured the artist who refused to give you his name, and brought him to you, to be properly punished for his churlishness. But I must beg you to deal leniently with him, as he is no other than Lawrence Wilmer, the son of the lad who first nursed your father when on the iceberg."

As she advanced towards me, I fairly gasped. I had not recognised the elder lady, —her step-mother ; but I could not be wrong in identifying Zöe with the subject of my dreams, poems, and pictures in Iceland.

Zöe, on her part, regarded me with a look of almost stupid wonderment, for which, as she could not by any possibility have recognised me, I was altogether at a loss to account.

Looking round in my bewilderment, my glance chanced to rest upon the face of the step-mother ; the look of intense annoyance which I there beheld, did not serve to interpret to me the situation.

Quickly recovering herself, Amelia (for thus I shall take the liberty of styling her in future) said, in a voice but little corresponding with her recent expression of countenance, for it was bland to a degree,—

" Dearest Zöe, are you not exceedingly rash to venture into the presence of strangers in your weak state ? Dc be guided by me, and retire to your own apartments until we are alone. Pray persuade her, Christmas, to take my advice ?"

Neither father nor daughter took any notice of her pleadings ; but Zöe came up close to me, and, taking my hand, said,—

" We ought to have been friends long ago. Please let me date back and consider that we were so."

Then turning to her father, she said, still holding my hand,—

" Now, papa, darling, I am going to take off my new-found old friend to talk with him all by myself. When you want us, you will find us in my room."

And she actually led me away without suffering me to raise an objection against such abrupt desertion of the party. I caught, however, a glance of encouragement from her father, upon whose face there was a curiously mingled look of apprehension and gratification.

She did not utter a word until we had arrived at her own little drawing-room, and I followed her example. She told me afterwards that she liked me for that, as any other man would have talked all the way. Entering the room, she led me straight up to a picture-stand, on which stood some drawings which I was at no loss to recognise. They were my Iceland illustrations; one of them representing the incident of my beholding her out on the floe, making wild moan to the ice-locked deep.

" There !" she exclaimed, pointing to the stand, " I will say nothing to you, and hear nothing from you, until you have explained to me how you came to paint those pictures and write those verses."

Her eager look as she said this, impressed me with the idea that her mind was still suffering from the shock it had evidently received before her visit to Iceland. Doubtful how my answer would affect her, I led her to a sofa, and made her sit down before I satisfied her curiosity.

" I was in Iceland," I said, " at the same time that you were there."

" Then you saw me go out upon the icefield to drown myself, and come back without having done so because I couldn't find a hole ?"

" I must ask your pardon," I returned, "for the liberty I have taken in representing a scene which concerned you. Had it occurred to me that it would ever be recognised by one to whom it might give pain, nothing would have induced me to take it."

" You mistake me," she said. " Tell me how much you know about me ?"

" I know nothing but what my own eyes showed me in Iceland,—that you were good, and lovely, and yet unhappy ; and what I have learnt to-day,—that you are the daughter of the most admirable of men, and one for whom I ought to have an hereditary friendship."

" You may add, and the step-daughter and sister-in-law of a white demon."

" What! You are married!" I exclaimed.

" Yes," she replied, sadly. " I was in too great a hurry. But I am going to be unmarried. My heart has no place for the false. Oh, what a fool I have been! Even my father does not know all, or nearly all. He has brought you to me to be my old friend. Your works revealed you to me as a friend who knew and understood me long before we met. Now that we have met, I have with you all the confidence of old friendship."

I pressed her hand for a moment, partly in order to assure her of my sympathy, and partly to calm her excitement ; for I felt that she was not altogether herself. But I kept silence. Presently she continued,—

" You cannot imagine the relief it is to me to find one who can sympathise without chattering. Oh, that woman ! with her sharp-cut lips and careful elocution ! How could my father have been so blinded to her character ! But he is not a man of the world,—I mean of

this world ; and her art was supreme. She
got tired of practising it when married ; or,
rather, it was that she found it impossible to
be a hypocrite every hour and moment, and
marriage is such a revealer.   But I am afraid
it was all my doing.   I wished him to marry
her.   Her kindness to me was so artfully
contrived, that neither of us saw through it
until the mischief was done.   There was
always something about her that jarred on
us, though."

Not knowing what to say, I said nothing,
but felt that her antipathy, whatever its
object or its justice, was already shared by
me.

" Nothing can give me back what I have
lost," she continued, " or remove from my
life the evil flavour of the past.   Personally I
shall be free, on that I am resolved, and my
father will not refuse his consent, when he
hears what I have to tell him, much as he
hates divorces for any.   The law allows
divorce to those who are married under a
false pretence.   But how will it be with him ?
It is true that there is virtually a separation
between them, but I doubt whether even her

vileness will suffice to reconcile him to a divorce for himself."

"What ! is she not true to him ?"

" True ? Oh, yes, she is true to him, with all the constancy of a cold hard nature, scheming ever for its own ends. Stay, you are Artist, and therefore Observer. Did you notice the colour of her complexion and hair ?"

" I was struck by their amazing clearness and brilliancy, but scarcely had time to note more."

" Do you attach any importance to colouring, in relation to character ?"

" Yes, indeed. The addition or subtraction of a warm tint often makes all the difference between a true and kind heart, and a false and selfish one." And as I spoke I glanced significantly at her hair, which was of the warmest brown and gold.

" Well, this woman has the cold white hue that belongs to the latter, in her yellow metallic hair and clear skin. Oh ! the spectroscopists must be right, when they say that races and temperaments vary according to the metals which enter into their composition. For I am sure that an analysis of Amelia would reveal very strongly the lines indicating the presence of tin and copper, or whatever may be the constituents of brass. My mother had the rich warm auburn, though much lighter than mine. I know little of her, save that she had been reared in tropical Africa, and possessed a temperament so ardent and impulsive, that she found it impossible to tone herself down to civilisation-point. I have been inclined to think that it was the very contrast that led my father to make this last selection. For I know he had much unhappiness in the first."

" Then his second marriage was scarcely one of mere affection ?"

" He thought it was on her side, so well did she play her part. But he was as much influenced by gratitude, and consideration for me, as by any thought of himself. Oh, how I hate all the kindness she showed me, when I think of the calculating spirit which prompted it."

By the time we finished talking, I understood that Zöe and her father had been betrayed into alliances with Amelia Bliss and her brother George, who was much under her influence. The plan had been for the lady to ingratiate herself with Carol, by displaying such affection for Zöe, and such exquisite propriety of sentiment and manner, that he should think he could not entrust his daughter's education and introduction to better hands. During Zöe's childhood, Amelia had lived much at the house in Surrey, and at length, with well-feigned reluctance, and solely she declared for the sake of her darling charge, consented to become her step-mother. Even with the attainment of this great end, she did not at once throw off the mask, but waited until Zöe's affections had been won by her brother, and a marriage actually contracted. This latter event had taken place in Carol's absence in Africa, and without his knowledge or expectation, Zöe's feelings being worked upon by the brother and sister until they were beyond the control of her judgment. It was, however, only on receiving a message in approbation, purporting to come from her father, whom she worshipped, that she finally consented. The aim of all this scheming was, of course, Carol's wealth. Having secured, so far as was possible, a claim upon

this, their caution relaxed. Zöe perceived
that she was not loved for her own sake, and
Carol found that the fair exterior and plausible
demeanour of his wife were but masks to a
hard and insincere nature. The first indication she gave of being other than she had
hitherto appeared, was her reckless disregard
of accuracy in ordinary conversation. To
such a degree did she learn to carry this
fault, that it was, I have heard, no rare thing
for her audience to gaze from her to each
other in wonderment, as with precise verbiage and ostentatious affability she poured
forth utterances of which the falsehood was
too apparent to be glossed over by any other
term.

Indeed, she seemed at length to have no
other conception of conversation than as a
vehicle for boasting ; and, regarding the
slightest statement made by another as intended for a boast, she invariably endeavoured
in her replies to *cap* what had been said.

To complete my sketch, and dwell no
longer than necessary upon a hateful theme, I
may here add that, as the love of display grew
with the possession of means to indulge it,

there was no department of life in which she
did not endeavour to outvie all who came into
contact with her. The range and assurance
of her conversation demonstrated her preten-
sions to universal knowledge ; and no matter
what the eminence of the scholar who ventured to correct her blunders, the attempt
invariably terminated in a triumph for her,
achieved by sheer force of assertion. So
confident was she of the perfection of her own
wit, that she allowed none of her attempts at
humour to pass without being repeated until
not a person present could escape knowing
them by heart.

Her husband, after his first shock of amaze-
ment at the manifestation of these oppressive
characteristics, strove hard to be blind and
deaf to them. Observing with more pain
than surprise the gradual withdrawal of his
acquaintances, and even of his friends, from
any society in which she was present, he
endeavoured to show her that such displays,
even of knowledge, would be in the worst
possible taste ; but that when they were displays of ignorance, they were utterly intoler-
able to a refined and educated society. Her

way of taking the rebuke revealed an innate vulgarity of soul that altogether sickened him ; and in regard to anything that could be brought within the category of mere taste, he never repeated the experiment. His next remonstrance was evoked by her habit of indulging in utterances of the severest uncharity against any person whose reported conduct appeared to her to contain an element of ambiguity. It was with every nerve of his moral nature quivering with indignation, that he listened as she picked the characters of people to pieces, and ascribed bad motives for their conduct, or scoffed at all notions of mercy and forgiveness, even in cases where errors had been atoned for by years of repentance and well-doing. It was only when no longer able to bear the infliction, that he exclaimed,—

" Silence, woman ! Do not further blaspheme God's creatures by finding only evil in them. Are you so conscious of perfect rectitude in your own every thought, word, and deed, as to be secure in condemning all others ?"

" I am sorry," she replied, " to find that

you do not appreciate a pure and a faithful wife too well to address her in that strain. I will retire to my own apartment and leave you to your reflections. I cannot be humiliated by my husband, whom I only consented to marry for his own sake, and that of his— his—dear child. Oh! that I had retained my independence." And here she put her handkerchief to her eyes, and sobbed, delicately.

" Hear me," he said, sternly, " and lay to heart what I say. It is no matter for boasting to have the physical characteristic you call purity, when every thought and word is an outrage against every virtue of the soul. Infinitely better is the ardour of the fire than the chastity of the iceberg, for with warmth there is a possibility of life ; whereas, of the disposition you evince, there can come nought but utter death. My whole moral nature rises in revolt against the insincerity and hardness you seem to delight in exhibiting. Unless you amend, we must dwell apart."

It required all the knowledge I have since obtained of Carol's domestic history, to make me understand how such a monstrous union

as this second marriage could ever come
about. I can see now how that the very
nature of the difference between poor Nannie
and this woman contributed to mislead him.
He had no fear of any rude impulsive outbreak on the part of Amelia ; or of any thing
being said save that which was exactly the
proper thing to suit the occasion. Actress at
heart, cold, pitiless, and insincere,—many a
less fine, less suspicious nature than Christmas
Carol's might have fallen a victim to her
wiles, even without undergoing the long
and artfully contrived process of ingratiation,
whereby the father was made to believe that
in wedding her he was giving as mother to
his daughter one thoroughly proved to be
worthy of all confidence and affection.

My conversation with Zöe was terminated
by the entry of her father, whose face bore
an exceedingly grave expression. Zöe commenced pouring out her thanks to him for
having brought the very brother that she
needed, but stopped on observing her father's
face, and said to him in a whisper,—

" Has she been telling you ?"

" My dear child," replied Carol, " I have

come to take you and Lawrence to lunch. I
hope I have not left him here long enough to
tire you."

" Oh no," said Zöe, " he is just what I
want my friend to be. He lets me talk on
and on as wildly as my troublesome head
prompts me to do. And when he speaks, it
is all so natural and simple that it does not
tire me in the least. So different from
Amelia's fatiguing way."

On reaching the luncheon room we were
received with a glance of the keenest scrutiny;
but the voice and manner relaxed not a particle of their ordinary careful graciousness.
In consequence of Zöe's remarks I paid particular heed to her stepmother's complexion,
and was startled at noting the accuracy with
which she had, so far as I could see, detected
the secret of that lady's character. Probably
the marvellous contrast between her own
colouring and that of her foe, had unconsciously suggested the hypothesis. Zöe had,
in addition to the pure auburn of her mother,
just sufficient infusion of her father's darker
blood to give a rich Oriental shade to her
whole complexion. Her hair, as I have said,

had a basis of gold, but verged on a deep
warm brown; a hue which indicated a temperament that required all the larger brain
she had derived from her father to balance
the mighty impulses of her heart. She was
manifestly of a rich and *roomy* nature; and
incapable of a petty action or thought.

Amelia, on the other hand, had the aspect
of one from whose veins all the blood has
been drawn, and whose vitality is nourished
only by a cold colourless lymph. Pondering
on this peculiarity as we sat at table, and
comparing the lady's manner with the account
I had just heard of her character, I was suddenly struck by a certain look about her
which at once suggested the idea that, though
whiter of complexion than the Whites themselves, her blood was not purely white, but
contained a dark infusion, probably of Hindoo
or African.

Observing her closely, with this notion in
my mind, I came to the conclusion that she
was, either nearly or remotely, of Eurasian
descent, that is, a cross between an European
and an Asiatic. If this was the case, all was
accounted for; and Carol had brought his

misfortune upon himself, by failing to ascertain the breed with which he was allying himself.

The more I dwelt upon the characteristics
of his wife, as described to me by Zöe, the
more did I recognise the identity between
them, and those which mark the race of half-
castes that owes its origin to our ancient rule
in India. The physical beauty and moral
deficiency which are too apt to combine in
persons thus derived, seemed to have united
their extremes in the specimen before me.
When once I had arrived at my hypothesis,
every word, look and gesture served to con-
firm it. There was the cold eye, the hard, precise intonation, the watchful glance, the keen
ear, the fawning flattering tongue, the head so
flat at the top as to indicate the utter absence
of a moral sense, but having in front strongly
developed faculties of perception and imitation, and at the rear all its capacity for love
centred on self, and perhaps on one of its
own kind, but the latter through habit of
association rather than through tenderness or
affinity of character.

This, as I came soon to learn, was the

nature of the bond between Amelia and her
brother. He was the sole being beside herself for whom she cared; and their connection with the Carols was the result of a
carefully planned and well executed con-
spiracy. The sister had, by arts already indicated, gained their entire confidence for herself. The brother was regarded by Carol with
distrust, which out of regard for his wife he
refrained from communicating to his daughter. But his absence in Africa was taken
advantage of by both brother and sister, to
effect against Zöe what in former times would
have been stigmatised as a deliberate seduc-
tion. This crime, as an offence in the eye of
the law, has with us no existence, each sex
being, under their altered relations, held responsible for its own act. Morally, however,
the blame rests entirely upon the side which
takes advantage of the inexperience, and
warm feeling, and lack of protection, of the
other, to obtain under false pretences that
which would be denied were the facts fully
known.

Zöe's horror on discovering that she had
been deceived and betrayed, was based solely

in her own moral nature. Her unhappiness
on this score was sufficient without the added
agony of the social stigma once attached to
the hopeless victim of the seducer's arts. Society now-a-days accords to a girl under
such circumstances, either a passing laugh of
good-natured ridicule, or a smile of kindly
compassion, and bids her be more careful in
the choice of her next lover. Its serious reprobation falls upon the man. Thenceforth,
he has no chance of getting a decent woman
to accept him. The sex itself avenges its
betrayed member. The fact that I am able
to tell and publish this history of Zöe's
first connection, without doing her fair fame
the slightest injury, will, at least for those
conversant with social history, indicate the
enormous amelioration the position of women
has undergone.

The fact that Zöe was an inmate of her
father's house, and dependent upon him, imparted to her betrayal a degree of criminality
which would be wanting in the case of a girl
occupying a less private position. A woman
who in early life goes forth from the parental
roof to earn her own living and make her

own home, avows thereby her readiness to
take her chance in the conflict of wits, and
an offence against her is not regarded by
society with the same degree of reprobation
as if she had retained the inexperience and
helplessness incident to home nurture. There
is the difference that exists between luring
a lamb from the fold and pursuing wild
game.

The bitterness of Zöe's feeling had been
aggravated by her father's conduct when he
returned from Africa to find his beloved child
sacrificed to a man whom he deemed altogether unworthy of her.

" Could you not wait for my return," he
asked, " before giving yourself up wholly ?"

" Oh, my father," she had replied, " I could
wait, but he could not. They told me you
approved. I believed him to be good ; and
I—I—loved him."

This was enough for the tender parent.
He set himself to make the best of it. Perhaps after all, he was prejudiced, and there
was more good in Zöe's lover than he had
allowed. He would ask him to come and
live in the house, and give him a trial.

The test of constant companionship soon settled the question for Zöe as well as for her father. George Bliss soon manifested all the evil characteristics of his sister, with this addition,—he had not only basely treated a woman with whom he had been previously allied, but he had denied that any such connection had existed.

He was dismissed, Amelia vehemently protesting her own innocence of any intention to deceive, though owning that her regard for both parties had led her to desire and encourage their union. Zöe perceived, however, that the statements which had been made to herself did not correspond with those made to her father. But the question—who was responsible for the forged message which alone had procured Zöe's consent?—had remained undetermined. Worshipping her father as she did, the slightest hint of his disapprobation would have sufficed to keep her from yielding.

In their anxiety to be just to Amelia, father and daughter had somewhat receded from their position of hostility and distrust, and encouraged themselves to hope that the recent experiences would have a beneficial effect upon her character. It was while under the influence of this reaction that Zöe had made the trip to Iceland with her step-mother, during the summer that I was there. Since their return, Amelia's evil charac-teristics had reasserted their sway, with, if possible, more than the old intensity, re-ducing both father and daughter to de-spair.

The freedom with which I had been re-ceived by Zöe was altogether foreign to her character. Her mind, which had never re-covered from its first shock, had just been ex-cited afresh by a new discovery, which she intended on that very day to communicate to her father. She had been dreading the effect the intelligence might have in embittering his relations with Amelia ; and eagerly welcomed in me one whose presence might be of ser-vice. She had a twofold justification, she said, for at once trusting me wholly. There was the sympathy already revealed in my works ; and the fact that her father had never introduced anyone to her in the way he in-troduced me. His whole demeanour had said to her, "Zöe, he is one of ourselves. Recognise in him a long-lost brother." Even long afterwards, when completely restored to health, she would have it that I must have regarded her behaviour as deficient in proper reserve, and it required no little art on my part to soothe the distress she suffered on this score. Indeed, I doubt whether it was thoroughly cured until I had recourse to a somewhat extreme remedy. But of that it would be premature to speak now.

Amelia had hitherto, as I have said, received all the benefit of the doubt entertained as to her complicity in her brother's treachery. By Zöe's discovery, the doubt was removed. She had overheard in the garden a conversation between the pair, which convicted the sister of being the most culpable of the two, for it revealed her as the author and contriver of the plot, and forger of the false message. Zöe had resolved to relate the circumstance to her father on that very afternoon. It had been a question with her whether she should do so privately, or in her stepmother's presence. I advised the former, feeling that children, no matter of what age, should never be suffered to witness altercations, or even discussions, between their parents.

My advice was taken, and after lunch—which the scarcely suppressed excitement of Zöe, the anxiety of her father, who was ignorant of the cause of her manner, and the suspicious watchfulness of the stepmother, who struck me as looking on me as a possible obstacle to her brother's rehabilitation, made anything but a cheerful meal—Zöe took her father apart, and left me alone with Amelia.

I found myself haunted by an idea which kept recurring to me with increased force, namely, that Amelia was not altogether a stranger to me. But I could not recall a single circumstance in confirmation of it. However, we began to talk.

" The Blisses had a great name in India, once," I said. " You are probably descended from the same distinguished family."

I wanted to obtain an admission of her connection with that country, with a view to verifying my theory of her Eurasian origin; but I was too clever and overreached myself. My ascription to her of a distinguished an-

cestry set her off on such a flight of glorifi-
cation of herself and parentage, that I began
to feel myself in the presence of one of the
most elevated of human lineage. How many
times her family had proved the salvation of
our empire in Asia, how regal the blood
which flowed in their veins, how vast the
wealth they had lavished for their country's
good, how wise and courageous the men, how
beautiful and good the women, how eagerly
sought their alliance in marriage, and how
great the condescension of herself and her
brother in consenting to associate with the
ordinary folk of modern days,—on these and
numerous other topics flight soared above
flight until I was only saved from being over-
whelmed by the augustness of the presence
in which I sat, by suddenly recollecting that
there was no necessity for believing a word
she uttered. So well had she acted, that I
had totally forgotten the character Zöe had
given me of her. But now this came to me
in all its force, needing no further confirmation. Christmas Carol married to an ingrained liar! There could be no greater
tribute to her skill in mendacity, than that it

had baffled his almost preternatural insight.
I saw now the significance of his remark
when commending me to her to be entertained
by her creative and descriptive talents. It
was a sarcasm! Christmas Carol become
sarcastic! Here was another tribute to her
powers. She had turned the sweetest of
natures into bitterness. Truly he was right
when he said that she revolted his whole
moral being. Association with her was a
moral suicide. I saw but one means of rescue
for him. Under the old laws that would
have been closed. They forbade divorce
save as a premium on one sort of vice.
Under them Carol would have been chained
to this woman "until death did them part,"
all, forsooth, because she was "pure," or because he was so. Away with a word that can
be used to describe two things so infinitely
wide asunder as the respective purities of
these two. Worse than worthless is such
purity of body where the whole nature is an
incarnate adultery with all the powers of ma-
lignance. Amelia knew that Carol detested
the notion of divorce, and that the soul of
Zöe was the personification of constancy.

This conviction was the rock upon which her confidence reposed.

Of course, a nature like hers could not realise its own exceeding hatefulness in Carol's eyes, any more than Carol could all at once comprehend the extent of her vileness. She was too keen, however, not to be conscious of the gulf between them. But she consoled herself by the reflection that in case the worst happened and she was turned adrift, it would be with a handsome competence to continue her career elsewhere. A man in Carol's position, and of his character, could not, she argued, throw over one who had held such relations with him, on any other terms, whatever her fault.

A message summoned me to Zöe's room. On my way, I met Carol, who was going to take my place in the conversation with his wife. His face told me that he now knew all, and had taken his resolution. His words charged me to endeavour to soothe Zöe's excitement.

CHAPTER V.

THE same evening Carol, Zöe, and I returned to London. On the way, he apologised to me for having dragged me into his domestic affairs. He had been taken by surprise, he said, by the revelation which awaited him; but his daughter's discovery of the deliberate imposition which had been practised upon them, and of her step-mother's share in it, left him no option but to act at once. Of course the scene had been a most painful one. For the first time the wretched Amelia had found falsehood fail her. All was over between the two families. He had pensioned off his wife and his daughter's husband, on condition that they left him and Zöe absolutely free, and never again ventured within their range.

"And now, for the first time in my life," he said, "I thank God that he has made divorce."

Yet he presently added,—

"Had I thought it possible I could save her, I would have continued to endure, and not put her away from me."

She had owned, he told me later, that but for her conviction that he never would take that extreme step, she would not have presumed upon his forbearance, but would have continued to act her adopted character to the end.

She even had the effrontery to offer him at parting a piece of advice, telling him to be sure and keep her successor on her good behaviour by making the connection one of limited liability only. "We women," she had said, "who, having neither fortune of our own, nor the ability or inclination to earn our own living by industry, are dependent upon men, are obliged to enact characters which are not natural to us; especially with such men as you, my dear Christmas, who are made to be cajoled. For we have no moral sense, as you call it, of our

own, or at least, cannot afford to keep one ;
though we may affect to have one ; and even
to be guided by it, in imitation of you, that
is, until we deem it safe to throw off the
mask. Now that I have been so foolish as
to lose you by throwing it off too completely,
I suppose I shall have to resume it for a
while. I must not let my next success intoxi-
cate me in the same way. Not that I deem
myself, or my brother, to have failed entirely.
And I am sure you do not grudge our arms
such little spoil as they have won for us ?"

" Grudge it to you !" he had replied. " Oh,
no. You are fairly entitled to every shilling
of it. You have earned it hardly. Ah, how
hardly ! far more so than either of you know.
May it prove a blessing to you ! Farewell."

Before we quitted the train, the notion
which had been haunting me about Amelia,
made itself clear to me. I now recollected
that she had in early life been a member of
the Remnant, though not of my mother's circle.
None had known why she had quitted it ;
but the gossip about her had implied that her
perversion was due to her failure to obtain
all the credit due to the devoutness of her

demeanour. The character she had left behind was that of being a mere actress, who
had taken up with the most formal ritual for
the sake of the facilities it gave her for com-
pensating the lack of sincere piety by an
ostentatious parade of its outward appearance.

On my telling Carol what I had recollected
about her, he said that she had, in the very
beginning of their acquaintance, owned to him
that she had abandoned the faith in which
she was brought up, in consequence of the
emptiness and unreality of its formalism ;
and claimed his sympathy for the painful
struggles of conscience she had undergone,—
a sympathy he had unsuspectingly accorded.

" Perhaps, after all," he continued, " I am
unduly hard upon her. Had she been reared
in a less narrow system, she might have found
legitimate scope for her talents as a pro-
fessional actress. Whereas, under a regime
of repression, the propensity to falsehood has
eaten into and vitiated her whole character."

After we reached the Triangle, Zöe continued to be so painfully affected that her

father bade her retire at once, and sent for medical aid. He, too, was much depressed, and requested me to stay with him. We sat up together, but spoke little; a word now and then, at considerable intervals. He, like his daughter, preferred silent sympathy to that of the loquacious sort. His utterances, when he did speak, showed that his suffering was for humanity, not for himself.

" Two hearts, and two only, have I specially striven to attach to myself, and redeem by love. In what I have failed, I know not. Well, well ; better to think the fault is in myself, than condemn humanity utterly."

I ventured to suggest that, although we might find it very hard to admit that the Supreme may have an ideal for us which is not our ideal for ourselves ; yet, with so many types in the physical world, it might be that we erred in demanding that there be but one in the moral.

" Surely," he replied, musingly, " love is a fire that ought to be able to fuse and assimilate all."

I had no opinions myself. As Artist, my love had been for freedom and beauty. And

on such an occasion, and in such a presence,
I should not have propounded opinions if I
had been possessed of any. The sentiments
expressed by him belonged to the category
of feeling, and to one who feels, opinions and
arguments are impertinences. Placed as I
was, an expression only of sympathy was
fitting, and sympathy might well be exhibited
in following the train of thought indicated by
him. So, not in answer to his last remark,
but in pursuance of it, I said,—

" Yet, if all things proceed from love, it
would seem that love must really be the source
even of the differences which lead to our dis-
appointments. If the initial and final stages
of being belong to love, harmony, or identity,
it may be necessary that the intermediate
condition involve opposites and antagonisms.
It is as impossible to conceive of conscious
existence without differences and degrees, as
of a whole without parts, or life without motion. And if opposites of physical nature,
why not of moral ? In objecting to the
essential conditions of life, people really object to life itself. They would have the fruit
without the flower, or the flower without the

plant, or the plant without the soil, or the soil without the elements, or the elements without the activity which makes them contend, and mingle, and fructify ; in short, they would have results without processes."

" Forgive me," he said, "if I have suffered my mind to dwell on one of your earlier remarks, instead of following you throughout. You have unawares trodden upon the heels of a mystery communicated to me many years ago, in one of my flights into the Empyrean :—that with spiritual natures sex is the product of love, not the reverse as in the merely animal world. Without entering on the vexed question, whether in our own case the individual mind precedes and forms the individual body, it is clear that what I have said must be the case, if the absolute mind precedes the material universe. For, if all things have their origin in universal love, the sentiment of love must have existed prior to the manifestation which we call sex."

" So that what we call good and evil," I suggested, " may be as male and female to each other, between them constituting and producing life."

He smiled at this, and enquired to which category I assigned which function ; but I confessed myself unable to offer a rule on this point, and said that probably it is sometimes one and sometimes the other. Only, that on the theory of the attraction of opposites, in order to make a perfect marriage between mortals, the better the one side is, the worse the other should be. ·And at this he smiled again—but not, it seemed to me, as implying that he considered what I had said to be altogether absurd—and remarked that marriage assumed many forms. There were marriages of intensification, as in the spiritual world ; marriages of completion, as in the ideal world ; and marriages of correction, or discipline, as in the actual world. And here he sighed.

Some days passed before Zöe consented to see me again. Her father took her consent as a sign of amendment. The excitement which had characterised our first meeting, and under whose influence she had so readily made me her confidant, had quite passed away. In her present phase of re-

action, she took an exaggerated view of what
she persisted in regarding as her unfeminine
forwardness, and expressed herself as ashamed
to see me. I sent back a jocular message,
saying that if it would put her more at ease
to know that I was out of the world, I should
be happy to do her the service of quitting it;
but that I thought it a better plan that she
should convince me, by ocular proof, of the
extreme propriety of her demeanour when
she was quite herself. I could not, however,
help deriving a certain gratification from her
self-banishment. For the self-consciousness
indicated by her conduct seemed to me inconsistent with a merely fraternal sentiment.

As the daughter mended, the father lost
ground. Avenil urged a more active life.
His body suffered through his mind. Let
him occupy his mind with other things, and
all would soon be well. I was now a member of the Triangle, and saw much of him.
I sought to bring him down to the Conversation Hall in the evenings, but he shrank from
the general view. To me, there was an immense delight in the society of the Hall.

The cultivated intelligence, broad views, and kindly spirit which marked it, perpetually suggested to me a contrast with the sectarianism in which I had been reared. It was as if I had escaped from the stifling confinement and gloom of a vault, into the free air and light of heaven. It seemed so strange to me to find Truth regarded as the sole criterion of any statement, and not its agreement with the tenets of a sect.

The only society which Christmas Carol would receive was that of a few of his most intimate friends, and this in his own rooms. Suddenly he announced his intention of taking Zöe abroad for a change. When I heard this, I secretly hoped to be allowed to form one of the party. Either divining or sharing my wish, he said that he hoped on some future tour to have me with him ; but this time he thought he was best consulting the object of his journey by taking his daughter alone.

I thanked him for his thought of me at such a moment, and said that, while I felt toward him and his all the affection and confidence which result ordinarily only from a life-long

association, I sometimes marvelled at the
existence of such a sentiment on his part.

He smiled, and said,—

"I have known you longer and better than
you are aware of. Since our first meeting, in
the Alberthalla, I have never lost sight of
you. I know your faithfulness, and your
labour, and your patience, and how, out of
pure tenderness of heart, you strove painfully
to reconcile two hardly compatible duties,—
your duty to your parent, with that which you
owed to your own soul. I have seen you
tried, and found you true, and that before
ever you were aware that any eye beheld you,
save that of the Everlasting Conscience."

"You would scarcely award me the credit
of having laboured and not fainted, if you
knew all," I managed to say, my eyes swim-
ming and voice faltering, not less at his words
than at the recollections evoked by them.

"I know," he said, "and regret the ex-
tremity to which at one time you were
brought. It was owing to my own unparalleled engrossment just then, that I suffered you nearly to slip out of my reach."

Here he rose, and going to a cabinet, took

out a sheet of paper, which he brought and
placed in my hands, saying,—

" The loss of this saved you. Do you not
remember that it was the turning point of
your fortunes ?"

Glancing at it, I found it was the rough
draft of the advertisement my desperation had
prompted me to draw up, and which, I now
perceived, I must have dropped in the publishing office.

" You don't look at the other side," he remarked.

Turning it, I found there some sentences
which I had totally forgotten having written.
Sentences which showed that, whether specu-
latively or practically, I had so far familiarised
myself with the idea of suicide, as to sum up
the arguments for and against it. The conclusion then come to was, that in yielding to
the temptation, I should be giving my mother
the very unhappiness I was then sacrificing
myself to spare her.

" To have carried out the project there
contemplated," he said, " would indeed have
been a terrible waste of your time and powers.
But I am going to make a clean breast and

tell you all, even though you may resent my action as somewhat impertinent. I chanced to be in an inner room when you were conversing with the agent, and could not avoid hearing your indignant rejection of his suggestion of a mercenary marriage. Partly to spare your own feeling, I would not let you know that you had been overheard. I had always felt as a child to your father, and in turn felt as a father to his child. This must be my excuse. Zöe's attraction to you through your work was altogether spontaneous. I need not describe my satisfaction at finding who it was that had excited her interest. Your position at home made open interference impracticable. I was a black sheep to the pietists of the Remnant ; and to have revealed myself then as your friend, would have been to defeat what at that time was the object of your life. In all that the agent did, he acted for me. It is true that I then considered you wrong in not endeavouring to win over your mother at least to a comprehension of your principles and motives ; for I thought affection, truthfulness, and sincerity such as yours must sooner or later find an echo in every human heart ; most of all in that of your own parent. My own experiences, however, have now convinced me of the contrary, and shown me that you reconciled, in the only way possible to you, the conflicting claims of affection and of faithfulness to your own convictions. You and I alike may find comfort in regarding such absolute incapacity for sympathy as a species of insanity. There is an insanity which comes by training, as well as that which comes by nature ;—though too often the one but supplements the other, as in that which takes the form of a narrow sectarianism. You see I speak unreservedly to you, even as to my own son. Would that you could have indeed occupied that place !"

" Is it too late ?" I cried, startled out of my cherished secret by this utterance, and the emotion which accompanied it.

" Too late ? Yes, you are fit for something better than to be sacrificed to one who is about——"

He was unable to finish. His voice faltered, and tears ran down his cheek.

" Great heavens !" I exclaimed, divining his meaning. " I never thought of that. Poor,

poor darling, how terribly she must suffer in the thought."

"You think that but for that," he said, "you might have reciprocated her attraction to you ?"

"But for that!" I cried. "Aye, and in spite of that! I meant all that I said when I expressed my tolerance for the error that comes through excess of heart. Do not breathe a word of it to Zöe ; but suffer me, when this trouble is overpast, to strive to win her affection, and convert the brother she deems me, into the lover she deserves."

He looked his gratitude, and I added,—

"Would that I could believe it would comfort her to know that I, at least, am utterly devoted to her."

"Nothing can comfort her at present," he said, "save the assurance that she is not despised by others as she despises herself."

CHAPTER VI.

THE great work approached its completion. Already were hundreds of square miles of the Sahara covered with fresh water which had found its way from beneath through the excavations. The admission of the ocean would cover thousands of square miles, even right up to the point where the river which issued from Lake Tchad was bringing down its rich sediment to fertilise the shore of the new sea. Careful surveys had been made to ascertain the precise limits to which the inundation would rise, and all populations within those limits had been removed to a safe elevation. So broad and deep was the channel by which the water was to enter, that the spectacle of its first admission was looked forward to with much interest and curiosity. Already a town had sprung up at the entrance, and a spacious harbour had been constructed by means of extensive breakwaters. The Emperor of Soudan, mindful of his challenge to a race between his own engineering operations and those of his cousin, had confessed himself the loser, ascribing his defeat to the unexpected hardness of the rock to be pierced. He hoped, however, that even if his tunnel could not be extended to the Red Sea, it might still be utilised for purposes of irrigation.

The rock and soil left to serve as a barrier to the sea until the final moment of admission, were so cut and bored as to be readily carried away by the rush and deposited in the deeper hollows of the desert. The agency whereby the last obstacle was to be removed from the channel's mouth, consisted of a vast system of mines, which were to be exploded simultaneously.

The labour of supervising the final preparations had been most beneficial to Carol's health. He appeared to his friends to be once more himself. Zöe, too, had regained much of her old brightness and elasticity, though not until after she had passed through a most severe ordeal.

We went, together with a large party from the Triangle, to the opening ceremony. The assemblage of vessels and notables from all parts of the world, made the occasion one of unparalleled magnificence. Of course, Christmas Carol, as the projector and executor of the scheme, would under any circumstances have been the most conspicuous personage present. But his more than imperial munificence in undertaking and carrying through such vast operations at his own sole cost, and without prospect of ulterior gain to himself, and the world-wide reputation he had acquired for the singular benevolence, simplicity, and nobility of his character—in some of the ruder countries obtaining for him the credit of a supernatural origin—these, not to reckon his personal beauty of face and form, caused him to be the one person whom to have seen, was to have seen all, and to have missed, was to have missed all.

At a given signal, in sight of the multitudes assembled on land, sea, and in air, the mines were fired. A number of muffled explosions in rapid succession was then heard, and the whole mass heaved and sank and rose again, like the surface of a boiling fluid. Then from myriads of pores the smoke oozed slowly out, showing that every particle of the soil was loosened from its neighbour. This absence of coherence in the mass was presently demonstrated by a slight movement of the surface, in the direction of the channel. This was proof that the experiment had succeeded; for the movement was caused by the pressure of the sea against the mouth of the channel. A few moments more, and the intervening obstacles had been swept away, as the sea rushed, a broad and mighty stream, through the opening, and along its appointed course, towards the heart of the Sahara, that vast region, from which it had for myriads and myriads of ages been utterly divorced, but with which now it was to be rejoined in a happy union for evermore!

The success of the enterprise thus far being ensured, the Emperor of Soudan, as the next principal personage concerned, turned to Carol and tenderly embraced him, placing at the same time a magnificent jewelled chain about his neck, while salvos of artillery rent the air.

The likeness between the royal cousins was undeniable ; but, I was assured, not so striking as it had been. The Emperor was much the stouter of the two, and his countenance bore an expression indicative of a life of self-indulgence, and little calculated to win trust. At least, such was the impression it made upon me.

Then followed an outburst of music from bands stationed not only on the earth and the sea, but also in the air, their combined harmonies mingling with the rush of the waters as they hastened towards the longing desert in such volume as to suggest the idea that the level of the ocean itself must soon be sensibly lowered ; a rush that would continue for months, until the thirsty sands of the new ocean-bed were satisfied, and could drink no more, and every remote nook and corner of the desert filled up to the level of the Mediterranean itself.

The music of the bands then ceased, and a myriad voices, chiefly of the labourers who had been employed on the works, commenced pouring forth to a wild melodious chant, the anthem,—

" Return, oh Sea ! unto thine ancient bed,
Where waits thy Desert Bride,
With dust bespread,
And parching sand—
Her fount of tears all dried—
Waits for thy moistening hand
To cool her fevered head.
Return ! return ! oh Sea !"

The words were written by me without any idea of their finding publicity. But Carol took a fancy to them, and having turned them into Arabic, and had them set to music, he made their performance a feature in the proceedings of that great day. The final verse—that lauding the hero of the event—I ought to state, was added surreptitiously, and took him entirely by surprise. The whole was sung with vast enthusiasm ; the blending of the musical rhythm as it rose and fell, with the constant rush and roar of the flood, pro-ducing an effect altogether extraordinary.

Even with night the music did not cease. The whole of the parties who were afloat in the air, had made an excursion down the

course of the stream to witness its issue from
the channel, and diffusion over the low-lying
reaches of the desert. Music had accompanied us all the way, and long after we had
returned to our resting-place and lain down
to sleep, it might be heard in the air, now far
and now near, now high and now low, now
singly and now massed, as the aerial bands
flitted to and fro, ever maintaining their sweet
utterances, careering and wheeling over the
landscape like a flight of tuneful curlews.

It had been a question how best to dispose
of the vast quantity of rock and soil which
had been excavated ; and it was decided to
heap it in a mass near the interior end of the
channel, so as to form a foundation for a
maritime city. This city, it was urged by the
assembled magnates, ought to be called after
its founder. They accordingly fixed upon
the name it now bears, which will serve to
perpetuate the beloved memory to all future
time.

There was nothing to detain us longer on
the spot. The hot season was advancing,
and Zöe was still far from strong. Carol
invited me to accompany him and his daugh-

ter to Switzerland, where the best effects
might be expected from the mountain airs,
and where, as he said, I should find fresh
scenes on which to exercise my art.

CHAPTER VII.

IGH up on the slopes of the Alps, in green vales embosomed amid peaks, passes, and glaciers, inhaling new life with every breath, and new vigour with every step of our daily rambles, we passed the happiest days it had been my lot to know. Carol was much occupied in examining and tabulating the accounts daily received from various points in the Sahara of the rise and advance of the waters. And I worked hard at my painting, giving meanwhile lessons to Zöe, who had insisted on learning from me.

Thus constantly and intimately associated with her, and witnessing the abounding richness and fulness of her nature, I learnt to comprehend and appreciate the impulse which

prompts the true woman to rank her love
as supreme above all prudences and con-
ventions whatsoever. Her soul was a sea
which but needed some fitting shore on which
to break and lavish all the blessings of its
ineffable tenderness. Yet so harmoniously
was she constructed that it was impossible to
tell whether it was in heart or brain that her
ideas and impulses had their origin. Thinking and feeling were with her an identical
process. In short, in every respect of heart,
mind, form and demeanour, she was all that
I could wish a woman to be, save that she
seemed to be utterly unconscious that I was
not really her brother.

Much in her as I could trace of her father,
there was also much for which he could not
be considered responsible. Her colouring of
character as well as complexion showed this.
She was something more than merely the
feminine of himself, a difference not attribu-
table to difference of sex. It was on my
telling him the result of my analysis that he
gave me the history of her mother. I then
clearly saw that Zöe was the due resultant of
the compounded natures of her parents.

On my owning to him the disappointment I felt at her apparent inaccessibility to anything like the tender feeling I entertained for her, he bade me have patience, and not betray my passion by the slightest word or sign. " Nature," he said, " is the best teacher and guide. The healing of a wound cannot be hurried, for it is a growth that is required. A premature disclosure might put all back. Nothing can be done at present beyond making the conditions favourable to the growth we desire."

" Making the conditions favourable to the growth we desire." The more I pondered over this utterance, the more fully was the depth of the philosophy contained in it revealed to me. I saw too, that it comprised the ruling principle of his life. Nothing about him was too insignificant to illustrate it. He applied it alike to the regeneration of a planet, the development of a soul, and the cultivation of a flower. To bring out the latent in-dwelling Deity that he recognised as substanding all existence, was for him the sole end of the life worth living.

The phrase, "background of Deity," was used by him one day as, resting by the edge of a glacier, he called the attention of Zöe and myself to an exquisite little flower, which was flourishing there in spite, apparently, of the most unfavourable conditions of chilling ice and naked rock.

"See," he said, "how this plant seems to contradict all our theories respecting the necessity to growth, of the conditions favourable to it. Can you account for its flourishing in such a spot, Zöe ?"

"Why should it not," she replied, somewhat bitterly, I fancied, "when evil flourishes under conditions which appear to us to be favourable only to good ?"

"Succeeding so well, under such conditions," I suggested, "to what might it not have attained under more favourable ones ?"

"Thus do the life and character of each of us ever tinge our philosophy !" said Carol, with a smile of sadness. "But yours, Lawrence, is not in perfect accord with itself. The point is one which no man can determine. Who knows how far the discipline of uncongenial conditions serves to produce that which is best in us ? If I mistake not, you once admitted as much to me."

I said that certainly I had found, even in my work as an artist, a liability to be carried in a direction contrary to the influences prevailing at the moment. For instance, it was always in summer that I succeeded in most vividly representing the phenomena of winter, and in winter those of summer. It seemed as if there were a reaction against one's actual conditions.

"The ideal," he said, "is more to you than the actual, and requires the force of contrasts to elucidate it. It is often so in life and character, as well as in art. Yet, nevertheless, and in spite of all anomalies, it is our duty to make the conditions as favourable as possible to the best, even though we know they sometimes will fail to produce the best. For what is the beauty of this very flower but the result of conditions favourable to such beauty, enjoyed by its progenitors near or remote ? And what the evil which Zöe deprecates, but a survival from times, perchance long past, of the effect of conditions unfavourable to good ?"

" We should hardly have noticed this flower had we found it in a conservatory," observed Zöe. " Instead of reigning a queen of beauty there, it would be but a humble courtier."

Something suggested to me the ancient class-feuds, by which, prior to the Emancipation, our social system was disfigured. And I made a remark to the effect that if the elements were possessed of sentiments corresponding to those of humanity, we might find the soil, the moisture, the atmosphere, and the light, grudging the flower the very sweetness and beauty which it derived from them ; much as the labouring classes used to indulge in enmity against the wealth, culture, and refinement which were the noblest result of their own toil.

" Add," said Carol, " chiefly owing to the selfishness which once governed the distribution of those results. Those who had the power took all, and gave back nothing beyond what they were obliged. A veritable Jacob's ladder has been man's ascent, first physical, then mental, from the first step planted in earth, to the apex piercing the clouds. In each of his stages,—the struggle for individual existence, the organisation for conquest and supremacy, and the final one of combination for mutual advantage, such as the conditions so always have been the results. It is when the parts show themselves so engrossed by their own personal interests, as they deem them, as to be incapable of sympathising with and aiding the higher destinies of the whole, that a state of things is produced which contains the elements of its own destruction. That is my definition of evil."

I had long wished to know precisely what form the Universe had assumed in his mind, and I took this opportunity to make a remark which led him to give expression to it.

" Whatever the state or stage of existence," he said, " there must still be a mystery recognisable by the faculties of those who are in that stage. The ability to apprehend such mystery involves the passage to a higher class. And until we have such ability, we are always liable to be in some error respecting the things which lie immediately below it. My view of the higher phenomena of the Universe may be utterly in error, although I have taken into account all the facts which I have been able to find in those phenomena, and tried to generalise from them with an un-prejudiced mind. However, for the present, this is where I stand. Deity, which is the All, has put forth out of himself, as it were, the whole substance of which the Universe is composed, withdrawing himself into the background, and leaving each various portion to the control of certain unvarying rules. These rules constitute the Laws of Nature. Proceeding through an infinity of stages, these portions gradually attain a consistency and consolidation which render them incapable of relapse into a lower stage.

"That is, they become, as individuals, indestructible and immortal. But to be this, they must harmonise in their character and emotions with the great Whole from which they originally sprang. Failing to do this, by reason of discordant self-engrossment, they prove themselves unfitted to endure, and so decompose and become resolved into their original elements, their constituents re-mingling with the surrounding universe. It is thus that whatever is sufficiently beautiful and good continues, by force of its own attraction, to endure and grow; while that which is obnoxious becomes dispersed, and vanishes by force of its own inherent antagonism to the general conditions of existence. I like thus to think of the good as enduring for ever, and of the evil as being dissolved and recast in fresh moulds, to come out good and enduring in its turn. I say, I like to think this. I cannot prove that it is so. Though at present I see nothing that is inconsistent with its being so."

I ventured to remark that, at any rate, he had determined for himself the question between Theism and Atheism in favour of the former.

"Call it rather," he said, "the question whether the material with which infinity was originally filled, and of which, therefore, the universe is composed, possessed among its other endowments faculties corresponding to those of sensation, consciousness, and thought, *as a whole?* Yes, I do so decide it, at least for myself; and for this reason. If the organised and individual portions alone were capable of thought, they would be superior to the rest, and able to penetrate its mystery ; and so, a part would be superior to the whole. But the existence of mystery incomprehensible by the parts, demonstrates for me the superiority of the Whole in all qualities possessed by those parts. It baffles the utmost scrutiny of the most advanced intelligence of any of its parts. What but a superior intelligence can do that ? But, beyond these or other reasons, I have *feelings,*—feelings which compel me to the same result. It is a necessity of my nature to personify the whole, and to regard the laws of nature as but the thoughts of God. But I am not therefore unable to comprehend the stand-point of those who deem it most probable that, as in the individualised part, so in the Universal Whole, the mechanical and automatic should precede the mental and conscious. Let each be faithful to his own lights. Only the presumption which leads men to dogmatise is utterly condemned. Imagine anyone who possessed but a fractional knowledge of our natures and circumstances, claiming dogmatically to define one of ourselves ! Methinks we should resent it as a great liberty."

"Ah! father," cried Zöe, "this flower, pretty as it is, will not be among your indestructibles. See! it is drooping already. And, look! here is a worm at the core eating away its heart."

As she said this, I observed his whole frame shiver as with a sudden tremor.

Walking homewards he resumed the subject of conditions, saying,—

"When I think of the force that has been constantly exerted through myriads of generations, to compel men to hate liberty, to hate each other, and to fear the light, and how tremendous is the strength of hereditary impressions thus accumulated, I am lost in wonder at the marvellous vitality of the divine spark within us. That it should have survived those ages of falsehood and suppression, is to me the standing miracle of the world. You remember, Lawrence, our first meeting, and the effect your first lesson in English history had upon you? Well, will you believe it? there was a time when one of England's greatest and most trusted Ministers sought to conciliate a priesthood by excluding that very study from an university course. The people oꜱ England were then but half awake. But this roused them thoroughly. ' Perish,' they said, ' a legion of ministers, whatever our debt to them, sooner than thus curtail Knowledge and subordinate Truth in deference to that old serpent of Sacerdotalism, which has so long deceived the Earth.' Ah ! they were grand times, those that led up to the Emancipation. Of all the past periods of our country's history, it is then that I should have chosen to live. And the owls and bats who lived in them used to declaim against ' the decay of Faith !' "

So the summer came and passed.

CHAPTER VIII.

E were still in Switzerland, when the ear of Carol, ever on the alert to succour or to save, was caught by a cry of distress which came from Egypt. Famine was not yet actually in the land. It was the prospect for the next year that was so gloomy. July, August, had come and gone, and the Nile, which ought to be at its utmost height in September, had scarcely risen above its lowest point; and the lowest point that year had been below any ever before known. The failure was, thus, to an extent absolutely unprecedented. It meant starvation to millions. Already were the superstitious populace crying out that it was sent in vengeance for the attempt to redeem the Sahara from its ancient curse. That the

judgment was specially intended for Egypt, for consenting to the scheme of her hereditary rival and foe, the royal house of Abyssinia, was manifest from the fact that there had been no lack of rain to swell the Upper Nile and its tributaries. It was by a supernatural intervention that the due flow of the river had been arrested.

September past, all hope vanished. The river ought to have been now fast subsiding from its inundation. From the parched plains of Egypt and Nubia, teeming with their millions, rose such a cry as can come only from a nation which sees itself on the point of perishing. The heart of the world was stirred ; but ere its hands could act, a mighty aerial fleet despatched by Carol, and laden with food, dropped down, as heaven-sent, into the midst of the now starving masses. But the report, again reiterated, that there had been no lack of rain at the sources, induced him to take another step. He despatched a confidential scientific expedition by fast aero-motive to ascertain the truth of the statement, and the point at which, if true, the river ceased to fill its bed. The greatness of the distance intervening between the Nile and his excavations made it utterly impossible, he thought, that there should be any connection between the two regions to account for the river's failure. Perhaps some accident had occurred with the imperial operations to the south. The engineers had some time since reported that they had tapped several springs, the water from which was so abundant as to impede their operations. The tone of the Soudan, and especially of the Abyssinian press at this time, was so menacing and even exultant in respect to their ancient enemy, as to lead Carol to make strong remonstrances to the Emperor, and to represent that such uncivilised conduct seriously imperilled the country's prospects of admission to the Confederacy of Nations.

The report brought back to Carol excited his utmost alarm. His agent had first come upon the river at Khartoom, where the clear and the thick Niles join to form the great river of Egypt. He thought, by attacking his task at this point, to ascertain which branch was in fault. To his surprise he found that both branches had been filled to their usual height, so that the escape must be at some point lower down. On seeking to obtain information, he found himself utterly baffled by the ignorance, real or pretended, of the people.

Leaving Khartoom, he next dropped down upon the river at the point where it is joined by one of its most important branches, the Atbara, —about one hundred and fifty miles below Khartoom. Here he found the natives in a state of wonder and alarm at the extraordinary aspect of things. The branch had performed its duty as usual, but scarcely any water had come down the bed of the main stream. The people, little advanced in civilisation or in-telligence beyond their remote forefathers, were at first very shy of their interrogator ; but, by representing himself as allied to the food-commission for relieving the distress caused by the drought, he gained their con-fidence sufficiently to learn that they had attempted to ascend the river in order to ascertain the cause of its drying up, but were stopped just above Shendy by a party of troops who said that the government had issued orders prohibiting all persons from approaching the river beyond that point.

Now, between Shendy and Halfay, for a space of about fourteen miles, the Nile runs in a deep narrow stream through a defile formed by high rocky hills. A gloomy place is this, and one which the people of the country care little to visit. The precaution observed in respect to it, therefore, seemed all the more strange to our party of explorers. They knew that the Emperor was driving a tunnel from the Sahara to the Red Sea, but its precise course had not been made known, and the river's bed was here at least a thousand feet above the sea-level.

Having fixed the point of disappearance within a space of forty or fifty miles, and finding the passage barred, the explorers determined to proceed cautiously. By dint of liberal payment, they obtained the guidance of a native who knew the country well. Then waiting till nightfall before starting, they rose to a height sufficient to escape being seen, and proceeded slowly up the river, making careful observations with their glasses as they went along. They knew that about the

centre of the defile was one of the cataracts
of the Nile—the sixth—and for the sound of
this they watched. As they failed to hear it,
they gradually descended towards the earth,
to make sure of not missing it. The country
seemed utterly deserted, and no lights or
other signs of a human presence were to be
seen. They therefore became bolder, and
approached quite close to the river. They
thus found the place of the cataract; but the
amount of water that flowed over it was
so scanty as fully to account for the absence
of the expected noise.

Ascending a little further, a glare of distant
lights became visible. Seeing this, they rose
higher in the air, and continuing their course,
presently heard the noise as of a camp, and a
prolonged roar as of a mighty rush of waters,
but with a more muffled sound than would be
made by a cataract.

Pausing directly over the spot, they were
able, by means of the lights with which the
camp was freely illuminated, to perceive what
was taking place below. The guide soon detected a change in the aspect of the spot.
His description, added to the testimony of

their own eyes and ears, explained all. But at first he was too terrified to speak. Those below were demons, he declared, and not mortals ; for they had dug a hole in the world, and were pouring the river into it ! A further inspection made it appear that a gigantic dam had been constructed slantways across the gorge, and a cutting made in the base of the mountain on the western bank, at the lower end of the dam, and that through this cutting the river was flowing into a deep hollow, for only thus could they account for the roar of its passage.

To make quite sure, they descended upon the river at a short distance above the camp. Here they found the stream flowing full and free as at ordinary times. Then, returning to the place where it disappeared, they crossed the mountain, in order to ascertain whether it issued on the other side. They even went to some distance, but found no traces of it. A final visit of inspection was then made to the place of disappearance, and then it was determined to turn the aéromotive westwards ; for Carol had instructed the leader, in case he found himself at a loss, to proceed to the

camp at the mouth of the Imperial tunnel,
and turn his wits to the best account. He
gave him for this purpose the exact position,
in latitude and longitude, of the spot in question. First, however, they returned to Shendy,
and set down their guide, charging him for
the present, if possible, to hold his tongue.

In consequence of the mists which covered
the earth, and extended far above it, they
were compelled to rise to a great height in
order to ascertain their position by stellar
observations. Having at length arrived over
the spot for which they were seeking, they
returned towards the earth. Here, while still
far up, the sounds of music and revelry plainly
greeted their approach ; for sounds ascend
from the earth far more readily than they
descend to it. The camp was a blaze of
light. Coming near, they saw the Imperial
banner floating above a vast pavilion. The
sound of rushing waters, too, rose to their ears.
Everyone below was evidently too busily
engaged in carousing to observe them. They
would descend close to the earth and make
sure, before reporting to their employer.

There was no longer room for doubt. At

a distance below the camp, short, yet far enough to be safe, and a little to the side of it, where the ground sloped rapidly, was the mouth of an enormous tunnel, and from it issued a volume of water, so vast that it could only be supplied by the sea or a great river. To ascertain which of the two, it was necessary only to taste it. This was soon done. Letting down a vessel, they drew it up filled. The water was muddy, but perfectly fresh. But, listen, what is the meaning of the chorus yonder carousers are singing so lustily? The words are Arabic, and the music is rude. This is the burden of their song :—

" Rescued from the hands of robbers, welcome back, O Nile, to thine own kindred. No longer shall Egypt be fat with the fat of Abyssinia, but fed by thee the desert shall rejoice ; yea, the Sahara itself shall be turned into a garden ! Amen. Amen."

CHAPTER IX.

N learning these things, Carol despatched a telegraphic message to the Emperor of Soudan. It ran thus :—

" MY COUSIN,—

"Relieve, I pray thee, my mind, which is sore disturbed by an evil dream concerning thee. I have dreamt that thou art the cause of the dire calamity which has befallen thy neighbours the Egyptians, in that thou hast turned the Nile from its bed into the desert, and deprived them of the means whereon they have ever depended for their subsistence. Say to me, if thou canst do so truly, that this is but a dream, and that thou art not seeking to repay thine ancient

grudge against Egypt by returning evil for
'evil."

This was the answer that he received :—

" My Cousin,—
  " Peace and good-will from me to
thee. Truly thou art the best of dream-
ers in all respects save one, namely, that
thy dreams are not dreams, but realities.
What thou sayest is true. The Nile, our
Nile, has at length, and at my instigation,
abandoned the strangers whom for tens of
thousands of years it has nourished with sus-
tenance drawn from us, and has returned to
its proper allegiance. A wrong is not less a
wrong because it is ancient. What I have
done, I have done within my own territory,
and in furtherance of the welfare of my own
people. Every rectification of an established
wrong produces suffering for a time. Yet
even towards mine enemies have I acted
tenderly, inasmuch as I have left them the
rich and ample streams of the Atbara, wherewith by judicious contrivance they can sufficiently water their lands. But, even should

this old and evil Egypt utterly fail and vanish, there will not be wanting a new and a better Egypt to take its place. Already is the Nile depositing its rich soil upon the sands of the Sahara, and flowing, a noble river, to meet the sea wherewith thy godlike hand has redeemed and gladdened the desert. Come when thou canst to

" THY LOVING COUSIN."

" This takes away my last hope," he said. " In spite of the fact that the river at that point is at least a thousand feet above the level required for his projected tunnel to the sea, I had been trying to persuade myself that he had yielded only to the temptation of an after-thought. But this shows that he has deceived me from the first." And he handed me the message.

" The plea is a specious one," I said, when I had read it ; " but I suspect the Federal Council will have little difficulty in meeting it, whether by argument or by force. You must keep that to publish, in case anyone suspects you of being a party to the scheme."

" Suspect me !" he cried. " No, no ! I may

at least trust that I am above suspicion.
But your first thought has indicated one
course that I must take." And he penned
a despatch in reply to the Emperor's :—

" Cousin,—The argument which thou hast
used is as unworthy of thy head as the deed
which thou hast done is of thy heart
Unless the wrong committed against Egypt
be repaired, and that speedily, the Federal
Council will repair it for thee, and at thy
cost. Even I, who am now, partly for my
work in the Sahara and on thy behalf, a
member of that great tribunal, will give my
voice against thee. As it is, thou hast by
this act indefinitely deferred the admission of
thy country to the Confederation of the Nations. The barbarity of thy deed is incompatible with the civilisation required of its
members. What arrangement may be effected
in the future to secure an equitable division
of the Nile, after thou shalt, by careful hus-
banding and augmenting of its sources, have
increased the volume of its waters beyond
that which is required by Egypt, cannot now
be said. The duty required of me is more

urgent. I devote myself utterly to the rescue
of the millions who, through thee, are perishing for lack of food. The fortune which I
derived from thy crown jewels shall minister
to the preservation of that crown from execra-
tion and ignominy."

When I had read this, he said to me,—
"What I have done hitherto has been done
out of income. This emergency can be met
only by a sacrifice of principal. We will return home at once, and place Zöe with our
friends, and then go to superintend in person
the distribution of supplies in Egypt. I
think I read you aright when I take this to
be your desire."

Following his wont when a wrong was
done, he still sought to find pleas in miti-
gation of his cousin's act. Anything seemed
better than to be compelled to regard it
as a treachery conceived in the beginning.
But a consultation with his engineers showed
his hopes to be untenable. An under-
ground exploration demonstrated the tunnel
to have 'been raised above the level necessary for its declared purpose long before it

approached the river. The change of the stratum to be pierced, from hard limestone to soft sandstone, had greatly facilitated the operations, and the downward course of the water through many miles of the tunnel was so rapid as to greatly enlarge the channel for itself.

The memory of these events is too fresh to need any recalling by me. How rapidly the world's horror at the act of the monarch of the dark continent, and its consequences, was succeeded by the world's wonder at the self-immolation of him who determined to thwart that act and avert those consequences, is too well known to require description here. Christmas Carol determined to save Egypt by himself; not that he could or would dissuade others from aiding, but by his promptitude and the immensity of his efforts he anticipated and distanced all competition. Summoned by him, from all quarters of the heavens sped "argosies of magic sails," laden with the essentials of life, and dropping down with their precious cargoes in the midst of the hungry and grateful populations.

18—2

For a whole year must these millions be supported by such charity, even were the Nile restored in time to afford supplies for the year following. In spite of the danger he was incurring, the Emperor remained obdurate. Although knowing that a solemn appeal had been made to the Federal Council, he refused to restore the river, and sent an army to guard the dam and the entrance to his tunnel against the Egyptians. But, an army on the ground to withstand an army in the air! The idea would be madness. Carol, however, clung to the hope that it was madness, and not badness that had perverted the mind of his cousin; for it was upon this theory that he accounted for all the villains of history. Avenil's theory is the same, only he uses it to account for the saints of history. Urging this plea in arrest of the Council's vengeance, and eager to save life to the utmost, he requested that an aerial force, comprising a strong working-party, might be placed at his disposal, to be employed on a service known only to the Council.

His request was granted; and leaving me in charge of the food-distribution, the organisation of which was now perfected, he suddenly descended with the Federal squadron upon the camp at the dam. The event was as he expected. Not a man of the Imperial forces would risk an encounter. The first shell, dropped so as to explode over their heads, dispersed the entire garrison, and the miners of the expedition were left unmolested to work their will upon the dam and tunnel.

So vast and solid were the works, that it was evident their construction must have employed thousands of men for years. On one side, the mountain had been pierced to make way for the river, and on the other it had been cast into the bed and walled up with mighty rocks, to turn the river into its new channel. In addition to this, a tunnel of enormous dimensions had been hewn through the solid rock for scores of miles towards the desert.

The first thing was to mine the dam, with a view to blowing it up. This was no small task, but the expedition was equal to it, and having made preparations for a series of explosions, at a given signal the mass was so loosened that it yielded to the pressure of the water, and went rushing with it down the now open channel of the river.

So low cut, however, was the tunnel, that a considerable portion of the stream still escaped into it. The stoppage of this was a task of greater difficulty; and it was necessary to accomplish it solidly, so that on its next rise the river should be safe from a return to the tunnel. On the successful conclusion of the work, Carol rejoined me in Egypt, exceedingly broken in health by his wear of mind and body. Far more than from his tremendous physical exertions, did he suffer from the thought of his cousin's perfidy. His sensitive soul seemed to be struck to its quick, as by the fang of a venomous serpent. His illness assumed so serious a character as to make his immediate return home imperative.

In order to guard against a reconstruction of the dam, one of the vessels of the squadron was detached, with orders to cruise at intervals over the locality.

CHAPTER X.

EVEN when restored to the quiet of his own home, and tended assiduously by Zöe, Bertie, and myself, Carol failed to regain his lost health. Zöe manifested all the joy to see me that I could wish, but its quality was not of the kind I desired. Her demeanour continued to have the perfect frankness befitting a sister, but obstinately refused to take any other form. She gladly admitted me to a share in all the offices of ministering to her father, precisely as if I had been a born brother to her.

I, meanwhile, made my home with Bertie, becoming as much attached to him as does everyone else who has the opportunity. He had outgrown the liability to the sudden illnesses which so alarmed his friends a few years back, so that old age found him a hale and hearty man. Together we daily walked to and fro between the two houses, and from him I learnt many particulars of Carol's life which before were unknown to me. He was very grave about his "dear boy," as he always called him, and said that it was far more from a moral than from a physical shock that he was suffering.

Carol's own hopelessness of his recovery was a bad symptom. He maintained that his work was done, and had ended in disappointment. Hearts were harder than rocks. The latter by a little industry and skill were redeemable. The former resisted alike all influences of love and of friendship. How he had failed to win the souls of his wives, was already known to me. Now he would tell me all the story of the Emperor, and I should see what cause he had for despair. Twice had he saved his capital from the destruction it would inevitably have met at the hands of the Federal Council, besides heaping benefits innumerable upon him and his people ; but now no word came of repentance or sorrow. What was the meaning of the advantages with which he had been endowed, if their exercise thus resulted in ignominious failure ?

I adjured him to take a more sanguine view of things. He judged by too high a standard, even the impossible standard of his own ideal ; although the result had not been what his imagination had framed, yet for all others it had been truly immense. In any case, a beautiful example, such as he had set the world, could never be lost.

Referring to Zöe, he said that but for her he should be glad to be at rest. She needed some one to lean upon. What did I think of her ? Had the interval been sufficient to enable her to become herself again ?

I told him that I believed her to be perfectly recovered, only that she had taken a firm resolve to lead a solitary life. Her very frankness with me showed that she regarded all men as brothers.

" And you ?" he said, regarding me with a wistful smile. " Are you still of the same mind ?"

I assured him that, with me, to know Zöe was

to love her, but that I had repressed every
indication of the feeling, through fear of its
making a barrier between us if known to her.
" I sometimes," I added, " am disposed to
think she still regrets her severance from that
man, even though she would on no account
be again associated with him."

Avenil, who came at short intervals, went
away each time more depressed. " Never
before was I disposed to believe in a broken
heart," he said. " Yet I can find nothing else
to account for his state."

The doctor agreed with Avenil, but said
that Carol's was a constitution of which the
heart was the basis. To injure him in the
emotional region was to strike at his most
vital part. With him it was as if the body
were but a function of the mind, not the mind
of the body.

" Bertie, dear," said Zöe one day, "my
father tells us that he wants nothing but to
be at rest. Does he say the same to you ?
Is there anything that could be done to bring
him comfort ?"

" I hate to bring a pang to your dear

heart," replied the old man. "If you will know, there is one thing that preys upon him, but he shrinks from obtaining comfort at your cost."

"My cost! What is my cost to his happiness!"

"He says he would die in peace if he only could see you worthily wedded first."

Her lip, ordinarily so indicative of sweetness, curled with scorn.

"I worthily wedded! Bertie, have either you, he, or I lost our memories?" and sinking into a sofa, she murmured, "I worthily wedded! I worthily wedded!"

"Bertie!" she said, springing up again, "has my father fixed upon any 'worthy' man to be the victim?"

Catching his eye, she again exclaimed,—

"I see your—his meaning. No,—Lawrence Wilmer is too good a man for such a fate. Happily he has no such thought of me. He is a model of a brother, and I hope to retain him as one."

"My dear Zöe," replied Bertie, "there is no respect in which you show yourself to be your father's own child more than in your throwing your life away in remorse for the faults of others. Now, without being in Lawrence's confidence or secrets, I read him very differently from you. My impression is that he is longing to win your love, but fears by betraying his feeling to repel you from him, and so lose altogether the delight of your society."

While listening to this speech her colour changed rapidly, she sank down upon the sofa, and gasped as for breath. Presently recovering herself she said, speaking more quietly than before,—

" I think you must be mistaken about Mr. Wilmer's sentiments. I am sure he looks upon me only as a sister, and that a somewhat fallen one, whose due is compassion rather than love."

She said this with a formality which, as Bertie perceived, cost her an effort.

" Then at least the idea of his caring for you is not disagreeable to you ?" said the old man, hazarding a bold stroke in order to surprise her out of her secret, if she had one.

Zöe was silent. She could not contradict him, and she would not speak untruly.

" My darling child, this will make your
father intensely happy. May I tell him ?"

" Your imagination is outrunning your
facts, at least with one of the parties concerned," she replied, somewhat saucily, it
appeared to Bertie ; but he saw that her
eyes were brimming over with tears, and that
she spoke under an effort to check them.

" I promise not to betray you, in case I am
wrong about Lawrence."

" Oh, Bertie dear, you know my history. I
feel as if I had no right to let myself love
anyone, and still less to accept love."

" Well, I don't see it in that light myself,
and I doubt whether anybody else does ; but
that is all better said to your father, or to——
to——"

She stopped the rest by a kiss, and made
him promise again not to betray her.

Finding the invalid somewhat revived the
day following this conversation, Bertie took
occasion to speak of me, remarking casually
that he could quite understand that the presence of one so entirely devoted and trustworthy, must be a vast solace.

I shall not repeat the gratifying things said by Carol in answer, though they will ever be treasured by me as a precious testimonial. But Bertie went on to say that what he could not understand was, any young man being so much with Zöe without falling utterly in love with her. Now it seemed to him, he said, that nothing could be more fitting than that I should become a son to him in reality as I was in affection and conduct.

" Perhaps," said Carol, " he thinks he would have no chance, and withholds himself from speech through fear of offending her."

" I see the awkwardness of the situation," returned Bertie ; " but young men are too apt to let their diffidence interfere with the happiness, not of themselves only, but of those who trust to them to take the initiative. It seems to me so natural and probable that a girl should be attracted by a man of his stamp, to say nothing of his family associations with you, that I only wonder that on her part Zöe is not as much in love with him as he ought to be with her."

Cunning old Bertie ! Falling, unsuspecting, into the trap, Carol exclaimed,—

" Oh, that she were ! There would then be happiness all round."

" Yes, if he cared likewise for her."

" But he does ! he does ! We have often spoken of it together. She, however, seems bent on remaining unwed. I can quite appreciate her feeling," he added ; " she feels herself humiliated by what has already occurred to her, and shrinks from again loving, or allowing herself to be loved. She is not as the great majority of girls are now-a-days."

" She comes of a proud stock, I know," remarked Bertie dryly.

Carol looked at him inquiringly.

" I mean," he continued, " that she inherits a tendency to feel as much mortified when she has made a mistake, as if she had forfeited a recognised claim to infallibility. Now, I consider it true humility, when one has failed in anything, not to brood over the failure—life may be better employed—but to try again until one succeeds. One does that in learning a new game of amusement. How much more in the game of life !"

" Would to heaven she would try again, if

only for this once. Zöe united to Lawrence, my last wish would be gratified."

" Tell him to ask her."

" You think she will consent ?"

" I say nothing positively ; but I am following my observations. Even supposing she cares much for him, the ease with which he contrives to conceal his feeling for her, in time may come to disgust her. A woman is very apt to distrust a love that can so effectually hide itself. Further delay may ruin his chance altogether."

" My ever wise Bertie, pray how came you to know so much about women ?"

At my next interview with Carol, he spoke of his wish to see us united, and said that he almost thought it better that I should strain a point and ask Zöe, than delay too long. " You might even," he said, " do it under the appearance of consulting her, as on a matter in which both your feelings and mine were enlisted, but in which nevertheless we were anxious to defer to her wishes."

He was too ill and exhausted for me to think of following his advice that day. The weather was intensely hot and still.

Longing for the cool upper airs in which he had been wont to take delight he had given directions to have a balloon constructed, on the old gaseous system, but with all the modern improvements. It was to be kept captive by a line attached to a windlass in the garden, so that he might ascend and be drawn back at will. Avenil himself superintended the construction. The sick man's eagerness to have it finished, struck me as a hopeful sign, but Avenil and the doctor shook their heads. It was made of a material warranted to restrain the gas for an indefinite period from fulfilling its longings to mix with the atmosphere; and Carol struck us as almost whimsical in his determination to fit it with a variety of contrivances for which, under the circumstances, we could see no use. In these he was assisted by Bertie, who regarded the whole affair as an elaborate toy, but nevertheless gave his aid gladly for the sake of his sick friend.

On the first ascent he lay out so many hours under the stars, having mounted in the afternoon, that we were somewhat uneasy at his failing to give the expected signal for being drawn down. However, when at length he returned to us, he was so cheerful and invigorated that we entertained hopes that the balloon was to prove the best of doctors. This was on the day after he had suggested my making my appeal to Zöe.

On retiring to rest he said to his daughter,—

" I had a strange longing, Zöe, when lying up yonder, to cut my tether and soar away never to return. I think it was only the idea of leaving you alone and unprotected that restrained me. Would it, darling, be such a very great sacrifice for you to make to my comfort, to marry Lawrence ?"

I was at the furthest end of the room, and observed only that they were conversing in a low tone.

" I fear, my father," she replied, in a faltering voice, and looking very much abashed, " I fear that it would be too great a sacrifice to ask of—him."

" So that if he were ready to make it, you would not object ?"

" For your sake, my father, I would not be out-done in generosity."

A lurking smile revealed all to him. Kissing her fair broad brow, he said,—

" Then, should Lawrence likewise not deem it too great a sacrifice, and say as much to you, you will not take offence ? I should miss him greatly were he compelled to quit us. A repulse from you would be a sentence of banishment. Perhaps he had better keep silence, at least until I am gone ?"

" Nay, if he has aught upon his mind, I should prefer that he speak. Whatever the issue, we could still live together as—as we have done. I should not think so very much the worse of him, as to require his dismissal."

So they parted, Carol once more calling out to me his good-night as he left the room.

I rarely lingered after his retirement, and now was undecided whether to say to Zöe that which was uppermost in my thoughts. What served most to restrain me was the reflection that it might appear selfish to speak to her of myself and my wishes while he was so ill.

Looking up from the book over which,

while thus pondering, I had been bending, I
found Zöe standing before me, regarding me
steadfastly with her dark lustrous eyes.

For a moment neither of us spoke. Then
she said,—

"What is it you have been reading, Lawrence ?"

It was a book of dramas, of the Victorian
period. One passage had specially struck me,
though occurring in a play which was disfigured and spoilt by false history and gross
prejudices. I had been wishing to read it to
Carol, but refrained through fear of recalling
evil memories.

"Sit down here, Zöe, and look at this," I
said, making a place for her beside me. "See
how a poet of many generations ago wrote as
if he discerned the relation between colour
and constitution. In this play of *Charles I.*,
the unfortunate king is made to say to his
treacherous favourite,—

"' I saw a picture once by a great master :
'Twas an old man's head.
Narrow and evil was its wrinkled brow ;
Eyes close and cunning ; a dull vulpine smile ;
'Twas called a Judas. Wide that artist err'd.

Judas had eyes like thine, of candid blue ;
His skin was soft ; his hair of stainless gold ;
Upon his brow shone the white stamp of truth,
And lips like thine did give the traitor-kiss.'

Is it not a full-length picture of your step-
mother, that is, supposing the fairness to have
been of her white bloodless hue ?"

" Ay, and still more so of—— Oh, Lawrence, how could you remind me of him !"

" My darling Zöe !" I exclaimed, thunder-
struck at my own heedlessness. " I would not
have pained you for the world. I thought
only of the sister. You know I have never
seen George Bliss. To me he is but a phantom, though a phantom whom to secure your
happiness I would pursue to the world's end,
until I had driven him beyond the flaming
bounds of space ; ay, and will, Zöe, if you
will tell me that by inflicting such vengeance
upon him, I can ease your heart of but the
smallest pang."

" You would do so much for me, Lawrence ?
My father was wondering just now which of
us would make the greatest sacrifice for
him."

" Well, Zöe, I am ready to enter the lists

with you. What is to be the nature of the competition ?"

" I like what you said of George Bliss just now. It is a relief to me to think that you regard him only as a phantom. It will help me to banish my evil memories."

" Tell me, Zöe, do you mean that you really have been allowing the past to influence the disposition of your plans, and—and affections for the future ?"

" In what way do you mean, Lawrence ?"

" For instance, is it on that account that you have withdrawn yourself from society, and become to all intents and purposes a nun, holding yourself in so that no man, not even I, who almost live with you, would venture to speak to you of love—no matter how mighty the impulse—for fear of grieving and offending you ?"

" Yes, Lawrence, it is so."

" And why, pray ?"

" Because I am a woman, and have a woman's instincts."

" Then hear me, Zöe," I said, placing my hand upon hers. " It is because you are a woman and have a woman's instincts, that

you are absolved from all shadow of blame
for the past, and therefore from all cause for
unhappiness in the future.   It is because you
are a woman and have a woman's instincts,
that you are capable of putting love before
prudence, and lavishing all the wealth of your
nature upon that which is unworthy of you.
And, further, it is because you are a woman
and have a woman's instincts, even to this
extent of not despising wholly that which is
not wholly worthy your regard, that I pre-
sume to tell you that I love you, and to ask
you whether I may hope you will ever consent to bless my life with the gift of the only
woman I have ever loved or longed for."

She seemed very much surprised, and
said,—

"How long have you felt thus toward
me?"

The little book of my winter in Iceland
was lying on the table before us.   Opening
it at the verses beginning,—

"Why haunt me when I know thou dost not love
me?"

I told her that it began with the first sight of

her, and had grown ever since, the more I saw of her, until it had become an indispensable portion of my being.

"Oh, Lawrence, Lawrence, how happy this will make my father!" And her head bent forward until it rested on the hand in which I was still holding hers.

"Why, he has known of it all along."

"I don't understand. Known of what?"

"Of my love for you. That was not wanting to make his happiness."

"My dear, dull Lawrence!"

"You love me, then! That must be your meaning. Sweetest Zöe, how could you torment me so long?"

"Can you not divine? I thought you had read me thoroughly. Listen, Lawrence: if I did not love you, I wished, oh so earnestly, that it were lawful for me to do so. But I dared not let myself love an honourable and true man, or to let him love me. Spare my speaking. Can you, will you not see that I—I—felt you were worthy to have all the freshness of my heart and soul and body, and that I could only offer you the soiled, unworthy creature that I am!"

When ecstasy had subsided sufficiently to allow of conversation, I said,—

" My own precious Zöe, what a thing it is to have a higher law than that of the Conventional ! Here is your dear father killing himself for the lapse of another from an ideal that other does not recognise ; and his daughter destroying her happiness and mine, to say nothing of her father's, because she was not endowed with an infallibility that made her superior to the arts of villains ! Really, Zöe darling, such vanity needed such correction. Let us believe the discipline has been purposely provided for you. And now let me kiss away those tears, and we will go and tell your, nay, our father, that we have agreed that no sacrifice is too great to be made to his happiness, and are prepared for his sake to put up with each other !"

" Dear Lawrence, I love to be bantered by you. It proves your confidence in the reality of our affection. But you too, you know, have not been exempt from submission to a higher law than that of the Conventional. The Conventional bids us be truthful and honest under all circumstances. And you practised concealment and deceit to save your mother from pain. And you have never before told me you loved me!"

A gentle tap at his chamber door elicited permission to enter. Carol had not gone to his bed, but was reclining, wrapped in a dressing-gown, beside the open window, gazing at the starry heavens. Our unwonted appearance at such an hour, and linked hand in hand, told him all.

"I can have no delay," he said, "for I know not how soon I may be called away. I have been listening to the sweet voices up yonder, and they have come nearer to-night than ever before. This only was needed to enable me to depart in perfect peace. To-morrow, Zöe,—nay, I will not be so precipitate,—the day after, you will give me the right to call Lawrence my son?"

Presently he continued,—

" That Egyptian business has made nearly as great inroads upon my fortune as upon my health. One cannot keep so many millions of people for a twelvemonth upon nothing, you know. But there is enough left to make the wheels of life go smoothly. Don't go home to-night, Lawrence. Let me feel that you are, as my son should be, when he has a sick father, in the room adjoining mine. Yonder is Bertie's wire. Signal to him not to expect you back to-night, and the cause. He will rejoice even as one of ourselves."

CHAPTER XI.

"SO long as ye both do live, or love?" asked the lawyer, as he took from his bag a number of forms of marriage-contracts for us to make a selection from.

"Charms or chains?" said Bertie, gaily, putting the query into other words.

"Remember that the former are very liable to be galled by the latter," observed Lord Avenil ;—for all our chief friends were present to congratulate us and witness our union.

"It is quite true," said Mistress Susanna, with a significant look, "that people are apt to be kept on their good behaviour by the knowledge that a separation is easy."

"But it is not infallible, as I know to my—

gain," said Bessie, evidently on a second thought substituting the word *gain* for *cost*. She was always a favourite of Carol's, and more than ever since, in obedience to her heart, she had vanquished her pride, and returned to her husband.

" With whom does the decision rest ?" I asked of the lawyer.

He said that it is a matter of arrangement between the parties, the lady, if under age, generally being represented by her parents.

" My daughter and I waive all voice in the matter," said Carol from his couch, "and leave it entirely to you, Lawrence. We have agreed to accept your decision, whatever it be."

This put me in a position of considerable embarrassment. A marriage of the first class is soluble only for unfaithfulness, or some tremendous fault equally impossible of contemplation by one placed as I was, and this accompanied by all the horrors of a public investigation. On the other hand, the advantages of fortune and position were all on the side of the lady. In claiming such a marriage, I should be appropriating a life-interest in her fortune. I asked the lawyer to repeat his interrogation.

"So long as ye both do live, or love ?"

"I may be very stupid," I said, "but I fail to see the distinction. Do you see it, Zöe ?"

She left her father's side, where she had been sitting with her hand in his, and came and kissed me on the forehead.

"Thank you, Lawrence," she said. "I may truly declare that my life shall end with my love. I cannot survive a second failure."

"My dear Zöe ! I did not mean a bit what you mean. I meant that my love would only end with my life."

She did not kiss me this time, but sat down by me, and held my hand in hers. It seemed wonderful to me, now that I knew the mag netism of her caress, to think that I had been so long and so much in her society without learning it before. The readiness with which her nature opened to the sunshine of affection, showed how severe was the frost by which it had hitherto been closed.

At length, I said that my difficulty in coming to a decision depended, not on any positive sentiment of mine, but on the pecu

liarity of our respective positions. All the
material advantages being on the other side,
I did not consider myself entitled to consult
my own feelings and wishes as I should do
were I in a thoroughly independent position.

"I anticipated the dilemma," said my dear
Zöe's father, "and have endeavoured to provide against it. This, Lawrence, is a deed
of gift by which I settle on you a fortune sufficient to justify you in deciding according
both to your judgment and your heart. Mark
only that we do not seek to influence your
determination, but shall love and respect you
truly whatever it be. So far from that, the
fortune is yours whether you wed Zöe or not."

Somehow, my circulation seemed to have
become deranged. My head was feeling
dizzy, and my heart had taken to thumping
against my side in a manner that I thought
must have been audible all over the room.
And, what was yet more curious, it seemed
to me to beat in rhythmical time with the
words,—

"Let your heart speak, Lawrence Wilmer!"
"Let your heart speak, Lawrence Wilmer!"

More for the purpose of gaining time to

collect myself, than for any other cause, I asked the lawyer to repeat his interrogation once again.

"So long as ye both do live, or love?"

"For life!" I exclaimed, with a vehemence I was unable to control or to account for. "For life, or not at all!"

The cause of my perturbation has since become apparent to me. The contact of Zöe's hand, backed as it was by the intense desire of the whole abundant vitality of her nature, had completely magnetised me. It was the impulse of her blood that was circulating through my veins, her heart that was throbbing in my breast, and her wish that made in my mind the rhythm,—

"Let your heart speak, Lawrence Wilmer!"

She herself, however, was quite unconscious of the effect she was producing upon me, though she admitted that she felt while then sitting beside me as if her being was in some mysterious way identified with mine.

There was no mistaking the satisfaction

with which my decision, and the heartiness with which I had enunciated it, were regarded.

" My son, in very truth !" exclaimed Carol, first embracing me, and then joining my hand to that of his daughter. Even Susanna indicated her approbation, by admitting that no rule is without its exception, and remarking, —" Our dear Zöe's character is one that requires the constant presence and support of a husband. Indeed, she will have nothing else to occupy her." And the lawyer proceeded to select from his bundle a form of the first-class, for the signature of ourselves and witnesses.

The one drawback to our gladness was the illness of our dear father,—for so I shall now call him. And here it occurs to me that some of my readers may be at a loss to account for the change made sometime back in my manner of styling him, namely, when, for the familiar and affectionate *Criss*, I substituted the formal surname. This is the explanation. During the period prior to my intimacy with him, I knew him only through the medium of those whom a life-long and affectionate friendship justified in using the familiar and endearing abbreviation. Seeing him with their eyes, and hearing him with their ears, he naturally was for me the *Criss* he was for them. But when I came upon the scene and knew him for myself, I did not deem it meet to adopt the same familiar tone. If nothing else, the difference between our ages and positions made it unseemly for me to do so. Thus it is that from *Criss* he became in my narrative *Carol*, or *Christmas Carol.* I could not bring myself to use his conventional title of honour, shrinking as he himself did from it. And now that he has become my father, all other names are merged in that one cherished appellation.

Whether owing to his entering upon a new phase in his disease, or to a resolution to lessen our anxiety on his account during this first period of our union, he certainly manifested such an increase of vigour and cheerfulness as to fill us with hopes for the best. He insisted on my taking Zöe a short tour, and introducing her anew as my wife to the circle at the Triangle, Bertie the while occu-

pying our place by his side   The season
continued to be oppressively hot and calm ;
but the device of the captive balloon minis-
tered vastly to his relief.   He made Bertie
also ascend with him, and read his correspondence to him in it.   His best hours were
those thus spent aloft, and it was there he
obtained his most invigorating slumber.

Our hopes were renewed but to be disappointed.   We had not long returned, when a
rapid change for the worse set in.   He was
fully aware of its significance, and told the
doctor he should not trouble him much longer.
He conversed much with me in a tone that,
though low and weak, was full of gladness.
He told me of all his plans for the good of
mankind, and spoke much of Africa as of a
country whose welfare was especially dear to
him, notwithstanding the fatal return he had
reaped from it.   " I suppose you know," he
added, " that my cousin the Emperor, having
no heir, is the last of his line.   Happily, the
result of his reign has been to enable his
people to dispense with the monarchy, by
fitting them for the higher condition of self-

government. However, should they at any
time need a sovereign, the old royal blood
will still exist in a son of Zöe's. Not that I
think you would be wise to remind them, or
to avail yourself, of the fact. Successions and
restorations, founded upon an ancient prestige,
have invariably proved a curse to all concerned. The world must live its own life."
With regard to the Emperor himself, he
charged me to do whatever might be in my
power to lessen the remorse he might feel at
having contributed to his death ; though he
admitted, on the other hand, that it might be
useful for the people of Soudan to know the
truth. Thus might his death, he said, be of
more avail than his life. Some causes never
prosper until they have had their martyr.

" Such reflection will bring but poor comfort to us," I said, scarcely able to speak for
the fulness of my heart ; " though history
fully bears it out, even that of Him whom
of all men you have ever most loved and
cherished. It must be an additional em-
bitterment," I continued, " to know that one's
end has been compassed by the treachery of
a chosen friend. Yet, even the least fallible

of human hearts was forced to admit the existence of a 'son of perdition,' redeemable by no love, and to lament over his failure to save him."

" I suppose it ought to comfort me," he returned, "to think that, whereas He met with one, the traitors to me have been but two. That, however, is not the thought from which my comfort comes. I am unable to recognise any as a child of perdition. It is not given to me to fathom all moral mysteries, but I see enough to enable me to trust, and that not faintly, the larger, nay, the largest hope —the hope that at last, far off it may be, yet at last to all, good will be the final goal——"

I recognised the quotation he was too weak to finish.

Recovering a little, he continued,—

" After I am gone tell this to the Emperor, my cousin, with my love and pardon. Tell it, too, to her from whom I was compelled to separate. It is not the good who are to me a proof of the hereafter, but the bad. And that, not for their chastisement, but for their amendment : that is, their development, the development in them of the moral sense—

that divine spark, of whose marvellous vitality we have before spoken — a development necessary, one would suppose, for His own satisfaction, as well as for their benefit. That is, if like man, He hates leaving any portion of his work unfinished."

Zöe and I sat much by his couch watching the face with the divine eyes closed, and often detecting no appearance of breathing; but there was ever over all the smile of intense peace.

More than once we thought him gone, when he returned to consciousness with ideas which seemed freshly gathered from the communion of saints. Once we thought he was wandering in mind, for we discerned amid his murmurings words that seemed to us utterly irrelevant. But presently his wan face lit up joyously, and he exclaimed in a voice of more than his wonted power,—

" Yes! yes! It is indeed encouraging. To what may not life come, when we see the progress it has already made!" An utterance to which Avenil afterwards supplied the clue, as well as its relation to the words which had struck us as so irrelevant. Those words

were *Aquarium* and *Zoological.* His mind
was running upon a conversation he had held
with Avenil on a recent visit to the institutions indicated, a conversation in which they
had made the objects before them the text of
a discussion on their respective theories of
existence and evolution.

The subject had evidently taken great hold
of him ; and it was with no little interest that
Zöe and I continued to listen to the workings
of his mind in relation to it, as he continued
his colloquy with the Invisible.

" All is clear now ; even the Justice that
was so dark and inscrutable. I see now that
the Universe is thy first thought, and not the
mere translation into fact of a thought already
conceived, and that in some way mysterious
to us, Thou thyself livest therein. But
thou seemedst to me sometimes to think
too slowly. I wanted heaven to be reached
at a single bound. Impatient myself, I re-
belled against thy patience. I could not
bear that men should themselves build the
ladder by which they might rise, toilsome
round by round. Oh, how I rejoice in
my conviction of thy inexorable justice, for

therein alone lies safety for all. Out upon
those who would divorce it from mercy, and
thrust themselves between. Thy justice and
thy mercy are one and the same. Oh, men
my brothers, what have ye not suffered
through that divorce ! The justice that could
swerve to one side could swerve also to the
other. But trusting the justice, ye cannot
but trust the maker of the conditions to be
content with the products ; seeing that it
would be injustice to make the products dis-
proportionate to the conditions. If the conditions have a right to exist, the products
have a like right. The poor soil and the
arid sky are as much a part of the universal
order as the rich garden, soft rain, and warm
sunshine. It is just that one should yield a
crop which the other would despise. It would
be unjust were both to yield alike. It is only
from those to whom much is given that much
is required. The worm ! the worm is one of
the conditions ; yes, Amelia, even the worm
that eats out the heart ! Nannie, darling !
are you listening ? and do you comprehend ?
See ! you have taught me something."

Speaking thus, he suddenly raised himself

and looked round with a bewildered air.
The sight of Zöe and me recalled him to the
present, and he said,—

"You believe, Lawrence, that the good
will ultimately prevail. You must revise
your belief, for it is wrong. The good is
always prevailing, though we may perceive
it not. Ponder this and you will learn that
from the very nature and definition of good,
it cannot be otherwise. For by good we
mean that which assimilates and harmonises
to the greatest extent its surrounding conditions : that which works in truest sympathy
with the essential nature of the rest. That is
evil which by its very selfishness arraigns the
rest against it. Good needs no power working from without to make it triumphant. It
triumphs by winning the sympathies of all to
work with it."

For sometime he remained unconscious to
all around, and murmuring words that were
hard to understand, though the voice was not
the voice of grief. After a while, either
through their becoming clearer, or our ears
being better trained, we learnt to comprehend
their import. While occupied one day in

listening to them, Bertie being with us,
Avenil appeared at the door, asking mutely
if he might enter. Beckoning him to tread
softly over the carpet, he approached noise-
lessly and joined the group. The murmuring
was going on, though so faintly as to require
close listening if we would catch its meaning.

Avenil bent down and listened.

" There is music and rhythm," he whis-
pered. " It is more singing than talking.
What can it be that he sings at such a
moment ? Methought I caught the words,
' Heaven the reflex of earth.' "

He was answered by Zöe, unconsciously using
the words of her father's favourite poet :—

" He sings of what the world will be when
the years have died away !"

" He leaves the world as he entered it : a
Christmas Carol to the last," said Bertie.

After a while his eyes opened ; and bright-
ened as they rested on Avenil.

" Master Charles dear," he said, using his
old boyish phrase for him, " I was wishing
for you. I want you to take Zöe and Lawrence back to the Triangle with you to-night.
Do not speak, please, but gratify me," he

added, turning his eyes to us. " I want this
night the repose of absolute solitude—solitude, that is, so far as this world and its
affections are concerned. I wish to be alone
with ——" and here his voice became in-
audible.

He was evidently bent upon it, and with
heavy hearts we obeyed him, first impressing
our kisses on his brow. Bertie was the last
to leave him, even as he had been the first to
receive him. We intended, however, to
return very early next day.

In the morning we were aroused by a mes-
senger bearing a letter from Bertie. It said,
" He is gone ; gone as he himself wished to
go. I remained with him awhile after your
departure. He appeared to rally, and asked
me to help him to walk across the garden to
the balloon. The effort of making those few
steps exhausted his strength. On reaching
the balloon he was forced to lie down in the
car. After a little while, it being quite dark,
he asked me to light a signal lamp, the pale
green one, containing Avenil's famous composition. Its brilliant light seemed to inspirit

him, for he declared he would go aloft, and have his sleep there. ' I think, dear Bertie,' he said, ' that I should die happier, if that were possible, did I know that I should for ever remain aloft in the land of dreams. Should, by any chance, the balloon escape with me, and bear my body upwards, do not send in search of it. Let it be, so long as the elements suffer it. A wild fancy you will think this, Bertie, but it is my fancy. Now kiss me, Bertie, and set the windlass free. Tell the servants to await my signal for hauling me in ; or if that does not come—and it may not, you know' (he smiled significantly as he said this)—'they may let me be till morning, unless the wind comes on to blow strongly.'

"As he finished speaking, he composed himself on the little couch in the balloon, in the attitude of one of the recumbent monumental figures in the ancient cathedrals, his face illuminated by the signal lamp, already looking like the face of the peaceful dead. I lingered, not liking to let him go where he would be alone and far from help ; but he cried to me, ' Now ! Bertie, now I am ready.

Let me rise!' and so with faltering hand I pressed the spring of the windlass, and suffered the balloon slowly to ascend. The night was intensely still. 'Perhaps,' I said to myself, ' the airs aloft will revive him once more, according to their wont, and the morning will bring him back better.'

" Alas, dear friends, I have to tell you that the morning failed to bring him back at all !

" I had gone into the house to lie down just as I was, keeping my face upturned to the window whence I could see the light of his signal lamp. I am old, and I was weary and heavy with sadness, and I suppose I dropped asleep. But on waking I could no longer see the light. Calling one of his attendants, I enquired whether he could see it. for it might be that there was a mist either in the air or in my eyes. He said that either it must have gone out, or else the balloon had escaped.

" Hastening into the garden, I stumbled over what proved to be a coil of rope. The man reached the windlass, and cried that it was indeed so, the balloon had broken loose, and his master was lost.

"At my bidding he brought a light, and we searched for the rope, over which I had stumbled. It was indeed the line by which the balloon had been attached to the windlass, and which now lay with its vast length in coils about the lawn. I examined the end, to ascertain whether the escape had been intended or accidental. There was no breakage : it had been regularly detached from its fastenings. I remembered then that the attachment had been made by an ingenious contrivance, which, while it was impossible to become loosened of itself, was yet capable of detachment by a slight pull.

"Dear ones, with whom I mourn as for a son prematurely taken from me, though this be so, there is no need to suppose that our beloved one hastened his own end. His latest words show that he contemplated the probability of his not surviving until morning : also that he coveted to take his rest in the clear upper airs rather than on the murky earth. I am convinced that, feeling his dying struggle upon him, he, in a final convulsion, withdrew the attaching bolt, and soared upwards, body and soul together. The vessel which bears him, a very ship of heaven, will never come down again ; at least, not in the days of any now dwelling upon earth. Nay, such is its extraordinary buoyancy—he would have it so, to steady it in the wind, while yet a captive—that, on being released, it must at once have shot far up into those rare strata of airs whither no living person can follow it, for death would overcome them long before they could reach the altitude where alone it will find its balance and fixed height.

" Let us, then, think of him we loved, not as mouldering in the damp earth, but as riding, even in death free and joyous upon the blasts he so loved to surmount in life, and sleeping the sleep of the righteous, or mingling with the pure spirits of his living dreams."

* * * * *

" Oh, Lawrence, Lawrence, can it really be that we shall see him no more ? that he can never again come down to us ? May not the fresh airs aloft revive him, as they so oft have done ? Ah, I see you have no hope, and that I must be resigned. But, oh, what a sense of perpetual unrest it gives me to

think of him lying out upon the breezes, subject to no conditions of regular motion or
speed, but evermore a sport to the most
capricious of elements. I have been longing
for night that we might sweep the heavens
for his pale green star. It is so calm that it
may yet be within range of the great Re-
flector in the Observatory. Come up and
search with me."

"Let us not call the element he loved so well
capricious, my Zöe," I replied, as we ascended
to the astronomical tower of the Triangle.
"None better than he comprehended the
secret of its impulses. The perfect sympathy
subsisting between the atmosphere and the
sun ; its responsiveness to every varying
thrill that expresses itself to us in heat, colour,
magnetism, light, was for him the most significant symbol of the dependence of the individual upon the universal soul. Born in a
balloon, I verily believe that by his own
choice, though the action of some divine instinct, he is also buried in a balloon. Buried,
as Bertie well says, not to moulder in damp
dark earth, but far above the corroding influences of our lower atmosphere ; far above

the lightning-ranges ; far above the breezes such as we know them ; even in those blue depths of air whence he was wont in life to seek his inspirations. Let us rather envy him his Euthanasia !"

"Ah, and if I thought that *they* would still visit him, and whisper to him of the Above, I should rejoice and no longer think of him as lonely. Believe you it can be so ?"

"Dearest, we cannot better honour his teaching than by emulating his trustfulness. Do you remember his saying that, as perfect love casts out fear, so perfect knowledge would leave no space for hope ? Zöe, let us cherish hope."

CHAPTER XII.

THE time that has elapsed since I commenced my labour of love, has been far longer than I anticipated. I hoped also to have given a much fuller account, and to have told it in fewer words. My principal difficulty has been to make a selection from the mass of materials which have flowed in upon me from all quarters,—materials of which each item is a separate testimonial to the excellences I undertook to exhibit.

For one reason in particular I rejoice that my work is finished, however imperfect and inadequate it be. It is a reason which would have had his eager sympathy had he lived. Already are the semi-civilised populations of Africa regarding him as more than man, and seeking a place to assign to him in their ecclesiastical calendars; not seeing, in their superstitious folly, that to claim for him a rank above that of humanity is to detract from his merits as a man. He himself would be the first to declare, could he have foreseen the occasion, that his sole miracle-workers were Heart, Brain, and Circumstance. "Love me, if ye will. Follow me, if ye can, in that which I have done well. But worship only the Supreme."

If this memoir achieve no other end than to show the peoples who seek thus to honour him, that they are thereby doing him dis-honour, and not him only, but the Creation in which he was a factor, I shall deem myself fully repaid. For I shall have done that which he would desire to have done, and done it in the spirit he would approve.

I trust that it will fulfil this end, and yet another also; and that the example here set forth will incite many to whom these days of vast accumulated wealth and enormous scien-tific appliance have given the power, like him to—

"Fly, discaged, to sweep,
In ever-highering eagle-circles, up'
To the great Sun of glory, and thence swoop
Down upon all things base, and dash them dead ;"

as sang his favourite poet of the Victorian
era, of one who might well have passed for
his prototype.

And for those, too, who are neither wealthy
nor learned, may he, without being summoned from his chosen rest in the deeps
of air, prove ever nigh in their hearts and
minds as a controlling ideal of their aspirations.

In his divine simplicity and comprehension,
the man himself was far greater than aught
that he said or did, or than can be said of him.
Of his principal achievement, I will only add
that the ocean-stream, whose first rush into
the Sahara we witnessed together, is now a
steady and equable current, just strong enough
to replace the loss by evaporation of the warm
and shallow sea which occupies the place of
the desert up to the very borders of the
plateau of Soudan. Already has this new
creation proved beneficial, to the climate of
the surrounding regions. Clouds heavy with

moisture now fling their grateful shadows, and freely pour their abundance on the once accursed plains. And no longer do the toilsome paths of the sandy desert whiten beneath the bones of its travellers, but above them speed the swift electric-ships and gladsome sails.

The moral victory is greater even than the physical. Jerusalem has avowed her share in the Emperor's deed, and is not ashamed to make amends. Avenil deemed it due to his friend's memory, and to international justice, to bring the complicity of the Jews before the Council of Federated Nations. The offence was held a serious one, for it was committed by one member of the Federation against another member. That the exasperation of Egypt has been allayed without exacting exemplary retribution, is due solely to the memory of him who sacrificed himself to avert her destruction. It is as a tribute to that memory that Egypt has consented to bury in oblivion her ancient feud with Israel, and to grasp in amity the hand of Ethiopia.

May it be that by the life and death of Christmas Carol, more than one *Eastern Question* will be advanced towards its final solution !

THE END.

BILLING, PRINTER, GUILDFORD, SURREY.

OPINIONS OF THE PRESS.

"We recognise in the Author of *The Pilgrim and the Shrine* an artist who approaches very near to the ideal that his brilliant pages disclose."—*Saturday Review.*

"One of the wisest and most charming of books."—*Westminster Review.*

"With this most clever author we feel a true and earnest sympathy. His life is a resurrection life, ever rising from the past to the present and the future. The book is talismanic, and, as Carlyle says of such books, will *persuade* men."—*Gloucester Mercury.*

"Accepting the Editor's disclaimer (of its autobiographical character) as made in all good faith, we can only suppose that the papers of a singularly gifted and daring mind have been put into his hands; unless, indeed, we give him credit for a power of imaginative realisation which, in respect of its descriptions of travel, surpasses the marvellous pictures of Mr. Kingsley in *Westward Ho*, and, in respect of his hero's processes of thought on theological, moral, and social matters, far transcends any psychological romance that we are acquainted with. Whatever the genesis of the book, it is a production of singular power and beauty."—*British Quarterly Review.*

"Its aspects are so varied, and the whole so fascinating, from whatever point of view it is seen, that we are forced to pronounce it a very masterpiece."—*Brooklyn* (U.S.) *Union.*

"We have found this to be a real and true friend, as every good book is; and we keep it near at hand, that we may, whenever we feel the want of a refreshing chapter, return to it.—*Boston* (U.S.) *Radical.*

"As to the literary characteristics of *Higher Law*, readers of *The Pilgrim and the Shrine* will not need to be informed that it is a work of more than mere cleverness. Something like genius inspires it. The originality of its conceptions, the penetration of its criticisms, the beauty and enthusiasm of its style, its careful study of character, and the ingenuity and independence of its speculations, will commend it to the admiration even of those who differ from its conclusions the most gravely."—*British Quarterly Review.*

"Those who have read *The Pilgrim and the Shrine* will need no words of praise from a reviewer to recommend to them a new novel by the same author. . . The method of *Higher Law* differs from that of the *Elective Affinities.* Goethe breaks out into a great deal of grossness. In *Higher Law* the absolute purity of the characters is the great charm of the story. There is a subtle vein of Pantheism —the physical Pantheism of Goethe rather than the spiritual Pantheism of Shelley—running through the whole story, and along with it are touches of a mysticism which reminds us at times of the fancies of Novalis. Considered as a work of art the unity which pervades the story is beyond all praise."—*Echo.*

"Unless the reader is thoroughly acquainted with the great questions of the day, unless he thoroughly, too, perceives the tendencies of modern thought, unless he is at home with the last Biblical criticisms, appreciates the lessons of Darwin and Huxley in science, and has laid to heart the doctrines of the more advanced school of physiologists, much in this very remarkable book will be perfectly unintelligible. Yet the book will find a large number of readers, who, as time goes on, are sure to increase. . . But the most superficial reader need not be frightened away from it. If he is capable of admiring wit and humour, he will find both in some of the minor sketches; if he has any love for description, he will find charming pictures of scenery in Mexico; if, too, he is capable of appreciating what true love means, he will find himself in a spiritual atmosphere such as we know of in only one novel of the present day. The whole of the love scenes are painted with an exquisite sense of poetry and delicacy of feeling. . . That same purity of style and earnestness of tone, that same depth of philosophic reflection which marked *The Pilgrim and the Shrine*, may all be found, rendered still more attractive by the beauty of the story, in the present work. There is no novel, in short, which can be compared to it for its width of view, its cultivation, its poetry, and its deep human interest . . except *Romola.*" —*Westminster Review.*

"To those who are averse to changes in our social or religious ideas, we may make for this writer the apology that he never disturbs any existing system without suggesting a higher idea in its room. Indeed, it appears, in his case, to be always the considera-tion of some sublime idea that impresses upon him the necessity of changing what exists. . . In *Higher Law*, we see conscience and inclination working in conflict, while all the circumstances are brought fairly before us, set, not in heightened colours or brilliant allure-ment, but clear and glowing, in a pure atmosphere. . . A bald outline is wholly inadequate to convey an idea of the sustained inte-rest and fine thought of this book. The plot is wonderfully worked out, with much subtle insight. . . It is to be hoped that a novelist of such rare qualities and originality, and promising such consummate excellence, will not tarry long before giving us another and another book with each maturer year and larger experience. But he will not come forward until he has something to say. . . In following his ideal as he sincerely does, in these commerce-ridden days, he deserves more praise than we know how to give."—*The Et-cetera Magazine*, for October, 1872, art. "Some Modern English Novelists."

"In the great flood of wretched cant upon this most sacred sub-ject (of marriage), this book seems to me inexpressibly valuable."—C. H. Dall, in the *Boston* (U.S.) *Radical*.

"Amidst the barren verbiage, the arid fruitless waste, which con-stitutes the plane of ordinary fictitious literature, this remarkable book is a sparkling oasis, where the thoughtful reader can satisfy the demands of both brain and heart. We have no hesitation in cha-racterising it as one of the most powerful productions of the day, a book that will make an impression on cultivated thought far deeper than the common ripple mark. . . Among the few notable examples in the region of fiction, in which it requires genius at white heat to triumph over all difficulties, are Goethe's *Wilhelm Meister*, and the *Elective Affinities;* Richter's *Flower, Fruit, and Thorn* pieces, and *Titan ;* Hawthorne's *Marble Faun;* and George Eliot's *Romola*. *Higher Law* is equal to any of these in eloquence and depth of insight, and in the art of construction superior to all except the last two."—*Chicago Times*.

"*The Pilgrim and the Shrine* describes with wonderful skill, vigour, and brilliancy the outward and inward experience of a young man of education who pushes away from his double home of country and faith, to seek his fortunes on the opposite side of the terrestrial and intellectual globe. The account of his travels by sea and land, of the customs he falls in with, the people he meets, the minds with which he finds himself in fellowship, the adventures and adventurers he encounters,—has all the charm of a romance, observation and reflection being so delightfully blended in every chapter that the reader's imagination is as much entertained as his eye, his intellect as much enriched as his store of information. And the story of his mind's journey from one region of speculative thought to another is narrated with an easy grace, that makes this most delicate and subtle portion of the book seem like the rich natural bloom, the fresh balsamic odour, of the ground over which the traveller passed. The author is so simple and rational in his methods, his purpose is so sincere, his heart so sound, his perception so true, that no gulf or crack is visible ; he carries his reader round the world of belief without a jar, and brings him in cheerful spirits to his journey's end without homesickness or fatigue. It ought to be a favourite book with 'radicals,' for it associates their views with knowledge, culture, elegance, wit, and imagination, disproving once for all the charge of baldness so often brought against them.

" The other book is, in some respects, even more remarkable than the first. The story turns on the fortunes of two young married people, whose personal characters, as individuals and as mutually related, as modified by circumstances and determined by temperaments, are probed and exhibited with the mastery of a profoundly thoughtful and deeply sympathetic mind. The book is a study of human character by purely rational methods, all conventional theories being put aside. The study is made on noble people in a noble style. The argument runs all the way on the uplands of the mind, where the verdure is rich, the horizon wide, the landscape varied, the air bracing, the frequent glimpse of river and hill superb; where the poisonous damps of the sunless valleys never come, and no stenches from the low morasses penetrate. The scenery of the book, natural and social, is magnificent. They who can appreciate its intellectual wealth will rejoice in its splendour. Such books are truly emancipating in their influence. They stimulate and instruct, entertain and educate. Products of a high culture, they create a respect for culture; and this is one of the crying needs in America."— Rev. O. B. Frothingham, in *The Index*, Toledo, O., and New York, February 8, 1873.

.